Buddha Wept

Buddha Wept

a novel of terror and transcendence

Rocco Lo Bosco

GreyCore Press

Book Design: Diana Lo Bosco
Cover Art: Shannon Beadle
Art Direction & Cover Design: Kathleen Massaro

LoBosco, Rocco.
    Buddha wept : a novel of terror and transcendence /
Rocco Lo Bosco
    p. cm.
    LCCN 2002114697
    ISBN 0-9671851-8-1

    1. Political atrocities—Cambodia—Fiction.
2. Cambodia—Politics and government—Fiction.
3. Mysticism—Fiction. 4. Buddhism—Fiction. I. Title

PS3612.O267B84 2003   813'.6
                                       QBI33-869

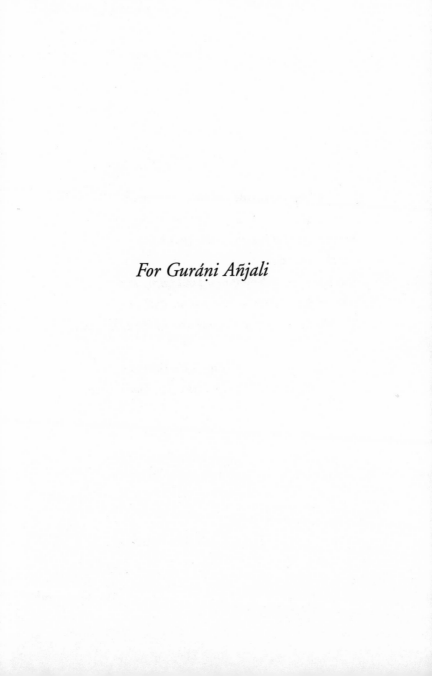

For Gurāṇi Añjali

Then there occurred what I cannot forget nor communicate.
There occurred the union with divinity,
with the universe....
I was one of the fibers of that total fabric and
Pedro de Alvarado who tortured me was another....
I saw the faceless god concealed behind the other gods.

—Jorge Luis Borges
Labyrinths, The God's Script

Autumn's Black Buddha

Last night's rain
left a thick mist
dreaming in the sunrise
coiling around the bases of trees
like smoke blown from the lips of angels.
Shafts of long slanted light
set the dying leaves ablaze:
yellows brilliant as the dawn's first
crescent of sun,
greens pulsating with hearts of emerald and jade,
reds, thick as blood,
bright as the lips of young women,
golds that agitate the longing
for a color that cannot be seen.

The towering choir of trees
chants soundlessly in the light
shedding leaves everywhere
like the pages torn from an endless text

whose meaning is to remain free of meaning.
Many find their way into the rain-filled pots
steaming beneath the trees, while a few
fall into the dark lap of Autumn's Black Buddha.

White Geese, Black Sky

Ona Ny was born in a city about twenty miles south of Phnom Penh called Khet Kandad. Her name came to her mother in a dream. Na-ren found herself in the midst of the dense jungle and a woman in gold, half-hidden by shadow, told her, "Your child's name is Ona. Do not forget, for she is consecrated." Na-ren believed this to be a very good sign and felt her family's life would be blessed. Her husband, a prosperous plantation owner and a self-taught man, did not want his children to struggle to learn as he had, and so he lobbied hard in Phnom Penh in order to have a small school built for the local children in Khet Kandad, communicating the seriousness of his intent with more than a few hefty bribes.

Ona grew up keeping company with Buddhist texts as well as some Western literature. One of her favorite novels was *To Kill A Mockingbird.* Her father had gotten her a picture book from America called *Bridges of the World,* and she had spent hours with it, utterly delighted by the great spans and varied architecture of the bridges depicted there. She vividly imagined being a bird perched on the top of the tower, gazing down on the road, the cars, and the mighty waters that ran beneath. She decided that bridges were among the most beautiful things built by human beings.

Avoiding the work her parents gave her, she often ran off to play with her friends along the bank of the river that ran past her village or at the edge of the forest. Even as a small child, she was haunted by visions of beauty. Occasionally, after cleaning fish with her mother on the river bank, she would find herself staring at the rainbow colors swirling on the river's surface. No longer feeling her own body or presence, she would become a point of light bobbing upon the restless water.

Once, on her way home, she saw a flock of snow-white geese pass under a black storm cloud. As the geese flew gracefully across the sky, Ona passed into an ecstatic trance and entered the soaring geese, seeing the sky all around and the earth far below, black clouds above like dark mountains and the wind an invisible river bearing her aloft. Joyously she dissolved into white darkness. When she opened her eyes again, the sun had nearly set and she ran home to her angry father who scolded her, saying that she had made her mother frantic with worry. She needed to keep her mind on worldly matters. "You are part of a family, Ona. And our family is part of much more than itself. Together we all keep the wheel of life in motion."

Kaypa Ny's anger with his daughter never lasted long, however, and after one of his rare outbursts, he would give her sweetened bread made from rice and sugar and speak to her in a soothing voice. "Ona," he would say, "you can't live with your heart in the sky. The world is very demanding. You must be strong and hard-working." Visions and trances were not uncommon in his country, though his daughter's spiritual gifts troubled him because they seemed particularly intense. Torn between pride in her otherworldly talent and fear that it would remove her too much from everyday life, he hoped her education and plantation work would provide a proper balance.

Ona's parents worked very hard in the rice fields and her father also made oxcarts, wagons, and plows. Everyone in the village respected the Nys for their intelligence, industriousness, and generosity. If someone were sick, Mrs. Ny would help to heal them with special herbs. If a friend or neighbor died, Mr. Ny would make their coffin. Ona and her brother Ket, her senior by three years, worked alongside their mother after they returned from school.

After sunset, they did their homework by lantern light. Ket was fond of getting Ona to do him favors by reminding her that he was responsible for her birth. The first time he told her this she became angry with him.

"I asked Ma to have you," he said. "That's why you were born."

"What do you mean?" she asked.

He shrugged. "I was lonely. I wanted a sister to keep me company."

"I don't believe you," she retorted. "Even if you were lonely, you would have asked Ma for a brother, not a sister."

He laughed at her and pinched her pug nose. She slapped his hand away. "Stop it!"

"No," he said, "it's true. I had a dream that I was flying over the tops of the tallest trees in the forest holding my baby sister's hand. That was you. I told Ma about the dream and asked her to have my sister. Ask her."

Her bright almond-shaped eyes burned with anger. "That's a stupid dream. You're making it up."

He smiled, elevating his already high cheek bones. "I'm not. I had the dream and went to Ma. Later I saw her make an offering at the altar. She was burning incense to Buddha and putting flowers all around. She was praying for you to come. I saw it."

"How do you know she was asking for me? How do you know?"

"Ask her if you don't believe me."

When she asked her mother if what Ket had said was true, Na-ren just chuckled and stroked Ona's face. "Ket thinks he's something, doesn't he?"

"Is it true what he said?"

"Ona, I wanted you here with us. And even if what Ket said is true, a child sent as an answer to a mother's prayers is a special gift to a family. This child enters the world through a golden door. Don't get upset by what your silly brother tells you."

"What does it mean that I came through a golden door?"

"It means our family is blessed."

But the thought that her existence sprung from her brother's loneliness bothered her. What if he hadn't been lonely? Then what? No Ona. She was here because he came first and was lonely. She was the result of his request. How stupid. Worse, she felt deeply indebted to him, since he was responsible for her birth; when he asked her to do his chores, she found it difficult to refuse. "Ma asked me to cut and clean the fish," he would say, grinning. "I have all these numbers to do. I hate cleaning fish. Please do it for me."

Cutting and cleaning the fish with a bitter frown on her pale face, her eyes narrowed in silent fury, she'd grind her teeth so hard that Ket would laugh as he came in the doorway. "What's the matter, little sister? Is the favor I ask too difficult for you?"

Once, when she didn't answer, he stepped closer. "Never mind," he said, reaching for the knife. "I'll do it myself."

She stepped back and glared at him, brandishing the knife.

He burst out laughing. "Come on, come on. You don't have to do it. Honest. I'll do it."

"I'll do it. I'm happy to do it for you!" she shouted, her face reddening and her frown so deep her mouth nearly made a circle with her chin. "Now go do your numbers and leave me alone."

"But you don't look happy."

"I'm happy. I'm very, very happy. Now go."

Still, she loved him intensely, and though he was older and a boy, she felt duty-bound to protect him. If he got into a scrape with another boy in the village, she would charge in and join the fray, though Ket would push her away and scream, "Go home. Mind your own business." But nothing he could do would stop her from standing by him.

She had a terrible time getting out of bed in the morning, and because Ket had to walk her to school, she often made him late. Their mother already in the field, he would shake his sister and yell at her, but she would sit on the bed rubbing her eyes while he put on his shirt and combed his jet-black hair. "You lazy banana," he would grumble. "Open your eyes. Get out of bed. Get dressed. Face the world."

She would whine, "I don't want to face the world. Why should I have to face the world? My dreams are nicer than school. Nicer than working in the fields. I don't like my stupid books. I don't like school. Why should I go? Why should I?" She hated waking up, going to school, struggling with letters and numbers flopping all over the lined pages like fish in the mud, having to keep her mind fixed on things of little interest. If instead her brother woke her to lie by the river and watch the clouds float in the sky, he'd have been hard pressed to keep up with her.

When Ket started middle grades, his new teacher was intolerant of lateness. He'd whack Ket with a bamboo switch and give him extra homework for tardiness. One day Ona's teacher sent her to bring a note to Mr. Koa and she saw her brother sitting on the punishment chair outside his classroom. "What did you do?" she asked.

He glared at her but said nothing.

"What? Is it my fault that you are punished?"

When he still didn't answer, she came closer to him and asked in a whisper, "Are you being punished because we were late?"

His beautiful black eyes narrowed and his handsome face darkened. His pursed reddish lips twisted with anger and she recoiled. "Yes, Ona. I am being punished and made to look foolish because I was late for school. I get punished nearly every day." He lifted his shirt and turned in his chair to show her the red welts on his lower back. "He aims for the ass, but his aim is bad. He says that I try to get away with it because our father helped build the school."

Tears sprang into her eyes. "Why didn't you tell me that the teacher was punishing you for being late?"

Ket's face further reddened and he clenched his fists and banged them against his knees. "I do tell you, you idiot. I tell you every morning that Mr. Koa doesn't tolerate lateness, but you don't listen. You're too busy rubbing your eyes and feeling sorry for yourself because you have to go to school."

Ona walked into Mr. Koa's class and went to the front of the room. The room fell deadly silent. Ona looked up at Mr. Koa and said, "Mr. Koa, I make Ket late. I'm the bad one."

Taking the switch from his desk, she began to beat herself severely on the legs, shouting and crying, "I'm the bad one, I'm the bad one, hit me instead!" Then she handed the switch to Mr. Koa. "Hit me instead of Ket. It's my fault."

Mr. Koa commanded in a stern voice that she immediately return to her class, otherwise she'd be expelled from school. Before the day ended, he leaned over and spoke softly to Ket. "You and your sister, you're a brave pair. But you'd better be on time if you don't want to feel the stick. Everyone must start school on time. No excuses."

The next morning Ket was surprised to find his sister washed and dressed when he awoke for school.

∽

When Ona was ten she made friends with a boy the other kids called "Blood Dog" but whose real name was Lido. Lido lived with an ugly brood of siblings in a dilapidated hut in the next village, situated on the far side of the market. A disgusting dog-faced child with skin red as sunset, he smelled badly and liked to crawl under the back of the old trucks parked in the marketplace to eat axle grease. An unshakable habit of grabbing at his penis made him appear even more distasteful. He would sometimes hold the tip of it through his pants with his thumb and forefinger, as if it might fall off if he let it go.

Ona felt sorry for him. After finishing her chores, she sometimes met him on the road between the villages and they played together, building houses out of branches from dead trees and exploring the forest for flowers and colored stones.

"What will you do with these?" he asked her once, fingering a particularly beautiful stone she found nestled beside a tree.

"I like to paint them," she said. "And you, what do you do with yours?"

"It's a secret," he said. "Maybe I'll show you some-time."

Lido was good at finding things too. He once found a long whip in the forest.

At first he and Ona thought it was a snake, but once they unearthed it fully they could see it was a thin black whip with a red handle. Lido snapped it and it flailed out awkwardly, the force gone before it even reached the tip. It took him weeks to get the hang of that whip, but he carried it everywhere, coiled in his belt. In time his proficiency increased and he could chop off the head of a little flower, or snap up a piece of glass glinting in the afternoon light.

After a while Ona didn't notice how ugly Lido was or how badly he smelled. She didn't care anymore that his family was so poor that nine of them lived in a hut designed to hold four. She didn't even care that he smoked cigarettes occasionally. She even tried a little axle grease and decided it wasn't so bad once you got past the texture of the stuff.

One morning Lido called for her early and said, "Would you like to see what I do with the stones we collect?"

He walked so fast that she became winded trying to keep up. "Slow poke," he called. "You walk like a turtle. Let's go."

Her heart beat quickly as she followed. What was he going to show her? What great secret might he have to share? Maybe he'd built a stone palace, or made brilliant designs in the dirt, colored stones in the shapes of faces or mountains. Maybe he'd befriended a beautiful animal who was waiting for him in the forest.

He took her to a rolling green field she had never seen before. The early morning sun spilled sky-gold across a blanket of little sweet smelling yellow flowers. Though the yellows and greens predominated, red, orange, and purple flowers were liberally sprinkled throughout. A slight breeze arose and the flowers rippled like the skin of a waking cat. The radiant colors sparkled in the light and the silky breeze carrying the perfumed scent played gently against her skin, causing Ona to struggle against the inward pull of ecstasy. She did not want to fall into a trance. She sat down next to Lido on a little hill at the edge of the field and bathed in the splendor. Honey bees buzzed, swarming over the delicious flowers, darting from one to the next, sampling the nectar. Bird song was rising up around them. She looked at Lido and said, "It's so beautiful."

"Yes, but that's not all. Come on," Lido said, smiling widely, sweat gathering on his fiery forehead. "I want to show you."

He led her to a small declivity on the other side of the field. Then he took a piece of cardboard out of his pocket and folded it in half. "This is a dragon mouth."

He swooped down on a bee that had just landed on a flower and crushed it in his cardboard instrument. "You have to be careful with this part. If I press them too hard, they die."

With the bee still trapped in the cardboard mouth, Lido walked to a little dugout beyond the edge of the field.

He dropped the crippled bee into a little hole that he had obviously dug before. "This is my bee farm," he said. "See the stone fence over there?"

She looked more closely. An extremely elaborate complex had been constructed from dirt, sticks, string, and the beautiful stones he gathered, a creation that must have taken him dozens of hours to complete and nearly as many to maintain each week. Little dugouts ran three times her height and several inches wide, decorated with stick fences and stone walls. Tiny huts had been constructed from straw and sticks. Elaborate string designs had been woven around twigs driven into the earth at various outposts around the bee farm. Lido had even made small guard towers out of wood scraps and sticks and had manned them with plastic soldiers. Hundreds, maybe thousands of bees filled this camp, many of them dead, all the rest dying, some with wings, some without. The ambulatory ones tried to walk up the sides of their encampments but stumbled back down.

Lido looked at Ona and smiled. "It's something, isn't it? I don't have enough time in the day to care for it. Some nights I come with a lantern while my family is asleep."

He picked up one of his bee prisoners and plucked off its wings. Flipping the bee on its back, Lido pulled off the legs one by one. A wiggling, furry, dark body, turned upside down, squirmed in the palm of Lido's hand. "See? Now it can't fly or walk."

He put the bee into one of the many small holes lined with tin foil dug at the edge of the farm. "This is an execution room," he told her, lighting a match, which he then put out on the bee's belly. "He's dead now," he assured her. "Would you like to try one?" he asked, standing up and pulling at his crotch. Ona noticed a little bulge in his shorts.

She looked at him and struggled for words. Finally she managed to ask, "Oh, Lido. Why did you make this? Why did you do this?" Her voice choked with anguish.

"It took me weeks, and I fix it every time it rains or when the wind blows hard. I'm going to make drain ditches with pieces of rounded bark from dead trees. Then I'll build some bridges as well. Would you like to help me?"

She shook her head, her eyes drawn to the swarms of suffering bees. "No. I want to go home now."

He was smiling over his creation and hadn't really heard her. "I want to make one of those things that chops off people's heads. I can make it using a razor blade that slides in a wooden thing. I can attach it with string."

When they left Lido's bee farm and the beautiful field of flowers, Ona had a bad headache and felt dizzy. She arrived home with fever and Ma sent her to bed. Days passed but the fever continued and Ma gave her herb drinks and put cool rags on her sweaty forehead. Whenever she awoke, she was haunted by two churlish thoughts winding around each other like snakes: why had Lido created the bee farm, and how could she have been his friend?

Late one afternoon she awoke to find her brother sitting at the edge of her bed.

"Ona, what's the matter with you?"

She looked at him and burst into tears. "I'm going to die, Ket."

His eyes widened and he leaned forward to look at her more closely. "Why do you say such a thing? You're sick, that's all. You'll be fine soon."

"No, Ket. I'm going to die."

His mouth tightened into a grim line and his eyes filled with tears. "It's not true," he exclaimed. "You will not die. We are to be together."

Then she told him about Lido's bee farm. Ket listened silently with his head down and his ear turned toward his sister, the side of his neck reddening as the story progressed.

"The suffering of the bees entered me while I was there," she said. "Now I'm dying too. Why does Lido do this to the bees? Do you know?"

"No," he answered, his mouth set. "But I have an idea for you to get well."

"What?"

"You have to get out of bed and come with me."

She put her hand to her head and winced. "I can hardly sit. Everything is spinning."

Ket grabbed her arm and his black eyes shone fiercely. "Ona. Don't be weak. We have to fight! Take me to the bee farm."

"What if Lido is there?"

"It doesn't matter. I hope he is."

"Ket, he really scares me."

"That doesn't matter either," he said, pulling her out of bed and helping her stand up.

When they arrived at the beautiful field of flowers, Ona's head began to spin again. She had to sit on a rock for several minutes before she could continue. Her brother patiently sat by her side. Then they walked to the bee farm, hand in hand, and his face turned with disgust when he saw what Lido had created. Ona began to weep.

Using his feet Ket began to level the farm, killing the crippled and dying bees. He turned to his sister. "Help me," he said.

"I can't."

"You must. Help me fix this."

Ona couldn't stomp on the bees even if they were almost dead. So she dug up some flowers from the nearby field and planted them into the soft mound of earth left by her brother's work. As she finished planting the flowers, he smashed the barricades and broke the stick fences in half. When they were finished, no trace of Lido's bee farm remained.

Walking back Ona felt no better. Worried that her sickness might now enter her brother, she entreated him to take her to the river. When they arrived at the shore it was nearly dark and she grasped his hand, asking him to walk into the water with her.

"No. You're too sick to go into water," he said.

"I must go in if I am to get well," she said. "Come with me."

As they walked into the water, Ona felt the river draining the poison from her body. She submerged herself fully and looked up toward the sky, a broken blur of violet and blue. She stayed under until she was out of breath and finally burst to the surface.

"How do you feel?" her brother asked.

"I'm not sure yet."

But as they walked, she began to feel better. By the time she arrived home, still soaking wet, she felt clearheaded for the first time in days.

She asked her brother again why Lido had created the bee farm. How could such a thing make a person happy? Again he said he did not know.

"There must be an answer," she insisted. "There must."

"He likes to kill bees."

"That's not an answer."

"He's a dog-faced bastard. That's why."

"Now Lido will come after me," she said, clutching

her chest.

"Let him," Ket said. "I'll fix him good if he does."

Next day in school Ket found Lido in the yard and told him about the bee farm. The two boys started to fight and as soon as Ket landed the first glancing blow, Lido's assault weakened. Soon Ket had him on the ground and Lido gave up.

"Stay away from my sister," Ket warned, pushing Lido's face into the dirt. "Don't talk to her or walk with her. Stay away!"

Days later, Ona was at the market for her mother. As she turned the corner to go home, she nearly walked into Lido. "Bitch," he muttered. "Don't think you're so big just because you have your brother. I'll get even with him. I'll get my turn."

"I'm going to tell him," she said.

He shrugged. "I don't care."

"Leave him alone."

"Why, what will you do? You're a coward."

Ona's face burned. "I am not a coward."

"Yes. Yes, you are. You ran to your brother. Who did it? You or him?"

"We both did it."

"I started another farm. See if you can find that one!"

Looking into his face, she would not avert her gaze.

She peered into his deep-set brown eyes to see if they would offer some clue. Though they squinted meanly at her, they said nothing about the bees.

She asked, "Why do you do it? Why do you hurt the bees like that?"

"I dream of things I can do with them," he said, sneering at her. "Things to build and arrangements to make it good."

His face looked ugly again, much worse than the first time she saw it. She'd forgotten how ugly he was. But his ugliness told her nothing about why he had created the bee farm. She now knew that people carried secrets within their hearts, and some of those secrets were terrible.

∾

Ona's visions ceased after the bee farm, and as she grew older she stopped missing them. No more would she rock with eyes closed while she listened to the beautiful inner music of flutes and drums and bells. No longer would she see a whirling funnel of light that began as a point within her heart and extended beyond the sky. She was barred from the golden seat at the crossroads where time did not exist.

Ona became skilled at artwork, fashioning strings of shells and stones hand-painted with detailed nature scenes. Though her time for painting was limited by her duties, her work became exquisite. She couldn't help but think that the gift of creating beauty on stones was a replacement for the lost gift of mystical beauty. And in a way it was a better gift, was it not? One could not share mystical experience. And ultimately if no one else saw what you saw, how could your vision be real? Not so with her jewelry and artwork. On a palm-sized shell, she could paint a forest picture so rich in detail and depth that admirers would claim that it might be possible to walk right into the scene. People came from surrounding villages to purchase her work. Her brother scolded her for giving so much of it away. For him, she made the finest piece: a shell on which a lone white goose flew beneath black storm clouds.

His eyes opened wide with awe when he beheld it. "The bird seems so brave, so noble," he whispered. "How did you do that?"

"I thought of you," she replied. "It reminds me so much of you. Strong and swift."

After Ona turned seventeen, she met a young man from a neighboring village. Eng Koy was fishing on the northern part of the river where it ran very slowly, and Ona sat in a small canoe with two girlfriends. The girls were fooling around, paying little attention to their direction, when their little boat drifted toward shore and tangled in Eng's line. The girls giggled as they struggled to free their boat from its entanglement, and Ona fell over the side of the boat and into the water. Eng quickly pulled the shocked Ona out of the water, and she frowned at him heavily when she saw that he was laughing.

Eng helped her onto the bank and they looked intently at each other for the first time. She was too beautiful for him, he thought. With her moon-colored skin, astonishing black eyes, and her thick waist-length hair, she looked like a true river goddess. Her wet clothes clung to her body and he could see in a glance that it was shaped like a fine vase. What emboldened him in that moment? Perhaps it was the vulnerability playing at the corners of her mouth, her struggle not to smile.

"Oh, what a lovely fish I have caught," Eng remarked with smiling eyes.

"Don't be presumptuous," Ona scolded, though a small smile finally broke through her stern expression.

"I apologize for my boldness," Eng said. "It's just that I think we will fall in love."

Ona looked away to hide her surprise. "Really? How interesting. A fortune teller."

"Oh, don't you believe in fortune tellers?" Eng asked. "Or are you too educated for that?"

Ona leaned over and peered at Eng's fishing basket. "Have the river gods smiled on you today?"

He flipped open the lid, and Ona widened her eyes in mock surprise when she saw it was empty. "Your fortune-telling skills don't help you much as a fisherman," she remarked, the corner of her mouth lifting in just the slightest expression of a smirk.

Eng folded his arms and smiled broadly. "My name is Eng. What is your name?"

Ona looked at her girlfriends, who stood back but urged her on with dancing eyes. "My name is Ona," she said, folding her arms in imitation of the handsome young man and returning his bold stare. Such staring was not common in their country; their daring candor gave the moment an auspicious flavor. Both were surprised by their own behavior as much as by each other's.

"Ona," he said. "Ona. That is not a Cambodian name. What kind of name is it?"

"My mother gave it to me. She says it means 'one.'"

"In what language?"

"In the language of dreams."

Eng began to show himself in Ona's village, bumping into her in the marketplace and at the edge of the forest. He secretly followed her and her girlfriends to the river and watched from behind the trees as they sunbathed. He saw her stand beneath a small waterfall that fell off the cliffs, her long black hair glistening with sunlit water, her dark eyes lit with an inner fire, and he declared her the goddess of his heart. Though she treated his advances with detachment, he felt that she would come to love him. He believed they had loved each other in many lives before and had only to awaken the memory.

He told her this as they sat on a green bench a few feet from the edge of a large pond where swans sailed with the ease of clouds drifting across the sky.

She laughed and shook her head.

"You don't believe in reincarnation?" he asked.

"What would reincarnate?"

"Our spirit."

"What's that?"

"You are a strange girl," he said. "Chantrea told me that you had many visions as a child. Yet you scorn rebirth?"

"I scorn nothing but doubt everything," she retorted. "A vision cannot be explained. It shows itself and does not care what we make of it. A vision is a secret which never really tells itself. But reincarnation is just a soothing idea. 'Oh, I will live on and on. I will not die.' Tell me, then why is everyone afraid to die?"

"I am not afraid to die," he said.

"Yes, you are. Let a big snake come before you and you'll run away as soon as anyone else. Don't be a fool and deny the fear of death. My Uncle Bo says that it sleeps restlessly in the heart and awakens at the slightest threat."

"See how wise you are, my dear? You speak like a sage. You must have lived so many times already. We have loved each other many times before, Ona. You love me. You just don't remember it yet."

She puffed out a breath, feigning annoyance. "Silly boy. If I ever love you, it will be because I will come to love you. My love for you is not a will be. It is a could be."

"Ah, you speak of loving me as if you already do. Soon we will be one, Ona. Just like your name. Soon, soon, soon." He reached into his pocket and brought out a silver box which he placed in her hand.

She took the gift with great hesitation, as if she wanted to give it back. But then she pulled at the silver wrapping delicately and slowly, shyly hooding her prominent eyes.

"Ah, you take so long!" he finally exploded, exasperated by her reserve. "I feel like pulling the box out of your hands and opening it for you."

She laughed. "That would ruin everything," she said, placing the still unopened box between them and taking his hand. "Opening a gift is always the best part."

"And why is that?" he said, pursing his lips and frowning at the box.

"Because we don't know what it is yet."

"I would think that knowing what it is makes the best part."

"That's because you're silly." She laughed, taking up the gift again.

The wrapping was off, and when she removed the cover, she sighed with delight. A delicate bracelet, its silver shaped in exquisite detail and its five polished stones gleaming like the eyes of an exotic sea creature, sat on a velvet backing. She removed it and placed it around her wrist.

"The old man Ko made it by hand."

"Oh, Eng. Ko is the best. It must have cost a lot."

"It is very small compared to my love for you. I want to send my brother to ask your parents' permission for us to get married. I think your parents like me anyway. What do you think of that?"

She took his hands in hers and pulled him closer. "Don't ask yet. Be patient."

Though pain stabbed his heart, he smiled. "You are smarter than I am and an artist too," he said. "You have many special qualities. Why would you want me anyway? I am only good to work and to love you."

"Silly boy. You said we've loved each other many times. If you believe your own stories, you've only to wait."

"I believe my stories. I want you to believe them too."

Ona shocked Eng by giving him a kiss, their first, very chaste, their lips barely brushing before she pulled away. A public kiss was nearly a scandal in Cambodia.

~

One rare day, bright and sunny during the rainy season, Ona and Eng were hiking with another couple along the trails that wound around some rocky cliffs and small waterfalls set in from the river.

Eng's friend Arun had received magazines on hiking and rock climbing from a relative living in France and had become enthralled with the idea of hiking. Eng laughed when Arun asked him to go.

"Hiking?" Eng said, chuckling. "What is this hiking? It's nothing more than walking around with a big bag on your back and going no place. Who has time for such nonsense? Hiking. Next the Westerners will make a fad out of blinking one's eyes. There will be a magazine devoted to it. It'll be called *Blinking*. Then the four of us can stand in the square and blink at one another."

"Ah, don't be a clown. The whole point is to do something different. Come on," Arun pressed. "We can get permission. It'll be fun."

"How will the girls get permission?"

"Ask Ona's brother for help. He can do it. And don't worry about Chantrea's parents. They're nearly senile."

Now, walking along and laughing with his friends, Eng thought that it wasn't such a silly idea, this hiking. He even thought it might be fun to follow Arun's suggestion that he and Arun climb down a very tall and steep rock wall on ropes, while Ona and Chantrea take a long winding trail around to the bottom of a waterfall where the four of them would meet.

The women were surprised when they arrived before the men, since they were supposed to have come straight down on ropes. Shielding their eyes with their hands, they looked up along the slippery cliffs. Nothing. At first their concern was mild, but when nearly a half-hour passed and there was still no sign of the men, Chantrea started to gnaw her fingers and Ona began playing with her hair. "What should we do?" Chantrea finally demanded, huddled over as though her stomach hurt.

Ona kicked off her sandals and walked towards the rock wall.

"What are you doing? What are you doing?" Chantrea shouted after her.

"They must have fallen behind the rocks above. I'm going to find them." She began climbing the rock wall quickly so she wouldn't change her mind.

"Come back, Ona. You'll fall!"

Ona kept climbing, hand over hand, grasping the jutting rocks for purchase. Even when the wall began to grow steeper, she climbed on, calling for Eng and Arun.

The men, however, were waiting for them at the bottom of another waterfall. Coming down on the ropes they had lost their bearings and were separated from the women by jutting rocks. They smoked and chatted as they waited for the women to come down on the trail. But then Eng grew impatient and suggested they walk around to look for them. Circling around their side of the jutting rocks, they saw Chantrea looking up at Ona, who was nearly fifty feet up the cliff face.

Eng ran to the bottom of the wall and called Ona's name, trying to keep the sudden terror he felt out of his voice. She looked down and saw him and he waved, forcing himself to smile.

"Looking for someone?" he yelled between cupped hands.

When Ona saw Eng at the bottom of the cliff, she felt a moment of sublime happiness. But then she realized how far down he was and that she no longer had any reason to be hanging off a cliff. The energy left her body like smoke from a smothered cooking fire. She took a shaky step downward but could feel her foot slipping. How had she climbed so high? Climbing down was out of the question. The wall was too steep; she'd fall and be smashed against the rocks below. Unable to climb down, she had no strength to climb up. The remaining wall stretched high above her, seemingly ending in the sky, which looked enormous, the billowing clouds bigger than mountains. The very top of the wall was covered with a slimy, slippery moss. Even if she gathered her strength, how could she possibly get past that?

She looked at her hands clutching the crevices in the walls and noticed the bracelet Eng had given her, quite worthless now. Her hands were tightening up and her arms ached from climbing. She looked down at Eng and called weakly. "Eng, I can't climb down."

Eng kicked off his sandals and started up the wall. "Stay where you are, stay where you are!" He climbed the rocks like a frenzied monkey. She thought of her mother, father, and brother. How upset they would be to see her like this. What a stupid thing to have done.

Soon Eng was beside her, taking deep breaths to recover and flashing her a forced smile. She was nearly panicked, frozen leech-like to the wall, her fear and stiffness quickening the fatigue in her arms and legs. She looked over her shoulder and down at the deep distance to fall. It gave her pins and needles in her legs and swelling ice in her belly.

"Ona! Look at me!" Eng demanded.

Slowly she turned her face to him. Tiger light flashed in his eyes. "This is easy. It's easy to get down. Just follow me. Okay?"

"I can't, Eng. I'm going to fall."

He inched closer to her so that they were almost touching. "Neither one of us is going to fall. We have a long life in front of us. See that bush growing out of the rock?"

She cautiously peered over his shoulder and nodded.

"I'm going to jump and grab hold of it. Then you're going to inch over and jump to me. I'll catch you and then we can crawl along the ledge till we reach that path. Do you see it? Do you see the bush?"

Ona's entire body trembled. How would she jump over into Eng's arms? And why assume the bush would hold his weight when he jumped? "I see it. You think the bush is strong enough?"

"If you were a bush growing out of the cliff, you would be that bush. I have complete confidence in that bush." He laughed mockingly, catching her by surprise and making her forget her fear for a moment.

"Okay, Ona. Steady yourself. I'm going first. Then you. Make sure when you jump, you do it full force. Put all doubt from your mind. Like this!" He leapt from his position, grabbing hold of the bush, swaying back and forth, his feet dancing against the slanted rock surface mid-air for a few moments before he pulled himself across and positioned himself on the ledge leading to the path so he could catch her.

"See," he said, grinning at her. "It's easy. Just move toward me until you can't go any more. That will be an easy jump."

Her heart beat frantically and she focused and began to breathe deeply. Eng waited, his sinewy arms extended. After a few moments she felt a little calmed and began to inch over. Some pebbles and pieces of rock slipped out between her feet but she pushed on. As she positioned herself to jump, Eng called out, "Jump with all your love."

She jumped with all her strength and he grabbed her easily, pulling her up and then hoisting her onto the ledge. He pushed her in front of him and in a few moments they found safe footing on the path leading back down to their friends.

When Ona related the event at the cliff to her brother, he beamed, telling her that Eng might be the man she would marry.

"Ket!" she said, becoming a little breathless. "Do you really think so?"

"Yes, I do. Marriage born of love. When it works, it's better than arranged."

"Do you think my marriage will be happy like yours?"

"I think it will. Yes."

She grabbed his hands excitedly, a small child again for a moment. "Oh, Ket, I feel the gods have really smiled on both of us. Sometimes it scares me. I feel my life is too abundant."

"Share with those around you, sister, and you'll have nothing to fear."

～

Eng's older brother, who since the death of their parents had raised Eng, approached Ona's father on his brother's behalf, asking Mr. Ny's permission for the couple to marry. Ona's father liked Eng. Though dark from too much sun, the boy looked wiry and strong with work-worn, large hands and piercing eyes that looked right into his. He could see the boy was honest and generous by the way he'd pitch in to do chores. And his eyes always softened when he looked at Ona. Mr. Ny granted permission for them to marry and arranged for a large wedding to be held in the center of the village, a festival of roast pig and seasoned vegetables, rice bread and chicken, saucy shrimp, stuffed flour cakes, cookies, and rice wine. The feast lasted two days, the night between lit by paper lanterns painted with bears, dragons, and tigers.

Finally the newlyweds made their way to their honeymoon suite, a small hut built at the edge of the forest, decorated with radiant flowers and small handmade lamps. The little room was sweet with the perfume of flowers, sticks of incense, sandalwood paste, and various scented woods mixed by Ona's mother. As Eng lay his bride back on the soft scented bed, he found her to be as shy as the new crescent moon teased by clouds. Her body stiffened and she became frightened. He kissed her and withdrew.

So nervous was Ona that her mouth became constantly dry and she could hardly swallow her food.

After a week, Eng entreated his wife. "Are you ill? What is the matter? Aren't you hungry?"

She was very hungry but too nervous to eat. "No, no. I don't eat much. You eat. I become satisfied watching you."

Eng continued to treat Ona with great tenderness. More than a month passed and still they had not made love. He had reached for her several times, but when she stiffened, he withdrew.

He stopped trying to make love to her but treated her no less kindly. When he awoke to the sound of her crying one night, he turned to her and asked what was the matter.

"We are not yet husband and wife."

He smiled at her and shook his head. "We are husband and wife. We are married. We will always be husband and wife."

"How can you be so patient with me? I am losing patience with myself. It's five weeks and I haven't let you touch me. I'm such a prude. I spoke to my mother about it. She's angry at me and said our marriage will be cursed if we don't have union."

"Because we haven't yet made love? Let me think about this." He mugged a pensive expression which made her laugh and he began laughing too.

"But what if years go by and nothing happens?"

"So wise you are at times, so silly at others. What would you say to such a foolish question? Something always happens, Ona. Even when moments go by."

"Now you're making fun of me."

"Without consummation, I'll have to find other ways to love you. You'll be my spirit wife."

His words made her feel as if a small bird were singing in her heart. It wasn't long after this that she took him into her arms and told him that she was ready. And, indeed, she was.

The Buddha Is Weeping

Eng built a house for Ona on high ground, above the threat of an angry river. It took two years to complete, a rare event, since most of the houses in the village were thrown together in a few days, their walls made from dried mud and braided leaves of river reeds, their fragile roofs woven from palm fronds. Ona's house had a cement foundation and wooden walls and a tiled roof, purchased with the extra money saved from several good harvests on the plantation. Everything else was made from the forest: the rough wood floor, the polished hand-crafted altar, and the painted staircase that wound up to the small second floor from the high porch. The house faced the river that ran on the east side, and some mornings the rising sun filled the couple's bedroom with liquid gold while other dawns brought a deep, intimate mist that pressed against the windows and muffled the morning calls of birds and insects.

Eng usually rose before sunrise, it being easier to work in the cool darkness than labor in the fields during the heat of the day. He and Ona grew rice and corn, beans and bananas, which they used for themselves, shared with neighbors, and occasionally traded; tobacco was their only cash crop and they sold it at the end of the harvest season.

Early in the evening, Eng and Ona would sit on their porch facing the river and chat as the locusts' shrill cries gave way to the chanting of crickets. Their small village followed the curving banks of the river, and the dirt lanes that ran between the houses were filled with children playing. When the river overflowed its banks and then withdrew, buckets of fish were caught in the ponds left behind in the fields. The plantation ran to the very edge of the forest.

Gazing at the river, Eng would occasionally ask, "Are you happy?"

"Shh," she would say, half-seriously. "Be quiet or the gods will hear you."

Gradually, the plantation became less fruitful. Several bad harvests and a disease in the tobacco crop made life difficult for Ona and Eng. Meanwhile they had three children: Ding-Toy, Tevy, and Kunthea. Ding, the oldest, was an affectionate but stubborn child and Ona fancied him to be much like her brother, not only because of his intense dark eyes and lean muscles but because he had a fiery yet loving temperament. Tevy was sickly and needed many treatments with herbs and needles. Kunthea, the youngest, followed her sister by a little more than two years. On the eve of Kunthea's birth, Ona's mother had a dream of a child seated on the shoulders of the Buddha who was dressed in warrior's armor, truly a shocking image.

"This child signifies great change," Na-ren told her daughter.

"Good or bad?" Ona asked.

Her mother turned away from Ona, hoping her daughter wouldn't see the concern in her face. "I'm not sure what the dream means. Maybe we should ask Bo-Som."

"You know what the dream means, Ma."

"Buddha dressed for war," her mother replied. "I feel this is not a good sign, especially in these times. The war moves closer every day. The vision is a bad omen, Ona. What else can I say?"

The dream preyed on her mind and Ona went into the forest to seek out the hermit, Bo-Som, who dressed in the saffron robe of a Buddhist monk. A spry man in his seventies, he was one of her mother's distant cousins. Ona and others from the village would occasionally go into the forest to seek his advice. Bo was greatly revered by the local people as a fully enlightened sage who reflected the light of a true Buddha. When she arrived at his ramshackle cabin, she found him outside waiting for her.

He took her hands in his and smiled, his misty gray eyes dancing. "Child. How long it is since I've seen you! How is your family? Is everyone well?"

She looked down at his gentle hands, very soft despite their wrinkled, veiny appearance. "Yes, everyone is well. I've come because my mother had a dream that troubles me and I want your advice."

His large dark eyes sparkled. "You need not visit me for advice only. You are gifted in spirit and I enjoy your presence."

"I have been very upset since my mother told me this dream, Uncle."

After she related the dream to him, he said, "The dream your mother had warns of times to come. Not only for you, but for all of us, the whole country." He sighed heavily. "There is still time for goodness. Family is the shelter of hope. Raise your children and do not fret about the future. Look to the steady sun and the ever-changing moon, the two sides of life. Enjoy your family. Live your life. But never forget you are just passing by."

"Worse times are coming then, Uncle?"

He moved his aged head from side to side and frowned. "Pain and pleasure follow each other continually.

Be still within yourself and watch the changes. If things get very difficult for you, imagine that you are dreaming a dream of flesh and blood."

"I must tell you, Uncle, that what you say is not consoling." She looked into his face and smiled. "Yet your presence calms me greatly." She handed him a package of rice cakes. "Mother made these for you." Offering him a sly smile, she added, "When you dream you are hungry, then dream that you are eating them. That way you can fill yourself again and again without actually eating them."

He threw his old bald head back and let out a belly laugh. Taking the package he said, "See how you are! You make such fun of me." Then he put his thin arms around her, drew her close, and whispered in her ear, "You are consecrated, child. Always remember that."

Following the birth of Ona's last child, the war intensified and political and social tensions increased in Cambodia as Prince Sihanouk struggled to keep his country out of the conflict. When he finally relented, giving refuge to the Vietnamese Communists who were allowed to land supplies in Sihanoukville and transport them to the eastern border, America began bombing Cambodia and the war moved past the country's borders. Those bombs, bringing fiery death to thousands of Cambodian people, paved the way for the disastrous changes to come, as Cambodia's

Lon Nol, aided by the United States government, grew in power, along with the opposing Khmer Rouge regime backed by Hanoi and China.

Ona and her family now scraped a difficult living from the plantation. Still the family thrived, though Tevy's health remained delicate. Ona's brother Ket had done well, becoming a local constable and fathering three children with his wife, Shon-Li.

Eventually Eng and Ona decided that the living made from the plantation was no longer sufficient for their family. They leased their land to a neighbor and moved with Ona's parents to Svay Sisophon, a town in northwestern Cambodia. They found a small school for their daughters and a secondary school for Ding, though both were inferior to the ones in Khet Kandad. Not quite a day's journey from his little sister, Ket would take his family for a visit once a month. His wife and sister would begin cooking together early on the morning of a holiday, spending happy hours exchanging recipes, garden tips, and of course, the gossip of their respective towns. They avoided talk of the war. Talk would make it more real, and no one wanted such a reality. Evening would come, always too quickly, and three generations would sit down to a feast. At these times Ona would recall Bo-Som's words: family is the shelter of hope.

Mother Na opened a small stall in the marketplace and Eng and his father-in-law became carpenters. After school Ding-Toy helped his father and grandfather, Ham Ny, who was still sturdy and energetic. They built a small house with a tin roof for the family, near the town's movie theater, where the roads delivered travelers from the provinces. Once her children were at school, Ona sat with her mother in a corner of the marketplace, behind a bamboo stand with a makeshift green and gold awning, and sold jewelry and pottery. The awning worked well against the rain, and afterward she would pour rainwater onto her hands and her mother's for a blessing.

Ona was disturbed by fitful dreams because, like many Cambodians, she was worried about the war. She had been nervous since she left the plantation, her nights no longer peaceful as they once were. Bombs were falling in Cambodia, far from Svay Sisophon, but that could change easily enough. Furthermore, a war was being waged within Cambodia between Lon Nol and Pol Pot. She tried to keep her mind occupied with other thoughts, but in the quiet of the night, thoughts of a troubled future whispered in the dark. What would happen if Pol Pot overthrew Lon Nol? How could she protect her family from the bombs? Where would they go?

About this time Kunthea, now nine years old, developed a rash on her stomach. The rash formed in the distinct shape of a hand with the thumb on the wrong side, a demon hand, bizarre and grotesque. This terrified Ona, and when the doctor could do nothing to help the rash, she took the child to see Bo-Som. When he examined the rash, his gray eyes widened in dread.

"The time of the enemy draws close," he said, tears brimming his eyes.

Ona began to cry too. "What is happening? What is happening to my child, Bo?"

He wiped his own tears and placed his wrinkled wet hand on Kunthea's stomach. "It will go away. Don't worry about the rash."

"What is it, Uncle? What does it mean?"

"Ona, now you must listen to me very carefully. You must learn to be deaf and dumb and teach the children to do likewise."

"But why, Bo? What are you saying?"

"Cultivate silence and teach it to your children. Be strong. Watch the demon pass, and pray. Pray every day." He crouched down and smiled into Kunthea's delicate face. Putting his forefinger to his mouth, he said, "Shhh" and smiled at the child. When she smiled back at him and imitated his gesture, he nodded and looked at Ona. "Silence, Ona. You must gather silence now. The silence will protect you from the enemy. That is all any of us has left. Do you understand?"

Ona nodded, the tears streaming down her face. She lifted Kunthea's shirt and looked at the evil rash. She wanted to ask what would happen and if anyone in her family would die, but she was too frightened of the answer. As she trekked back into the forest, she turned toward the hut. The monk was standing in the doorway waving to her, his sad face gray in the forest mist.

~

In late April, on a hot windless morning, the first soldiers from the Khmer Rouge arrived in Svay Sisophon on a truck. Smiling and leaning over the side railing of the steel bed, they waved red cloths at the people. Through a loudspeaker mounted on the cab of the truck, a soldier excitedly told the people to abandon all arms, for the friends of the people had arrived. Soon more trucks came and roared through the marketplace like excited bulls, making the dogs bark and bringing the people from their homes. The soldiers were boys, shouting, "Mother!" and "Father!" as a greeting of triumph to the people they passed. The people were happy and shouted greetings back, for they knew these boys under Pol Pot and the Khmer Rouge were patriots and sworn enemies of the corrupt and violent government of Lon Nol. The arrival of the trucks meant that the war between them had ended in favor of Pol Pot.

When the trucks stopped in the marketplace, soldiers jumped from them and strode onto the porches of houses and asked the people if they had any weapons. "You have no need of guns," they assured everyone. "A new order is being formed. We are here to protect you now. Relinquish your guns and pistols for the good of the state. We must forge ahead now as one nation, brothers and sisters with one goal."

Ona folded up her market table, brought it home, and hurried to the temple to pray. A shocked crowd had already gathered at the altar. The statue of Buddha was no longer smiling, but weeping, a deep frown on its stone face. Ona had to push her way through the thickening throng. Everyone spoke in excited and fearful voices. "The Buddha is crying. What can this mean?"

When Ona approached the idol and saw the tears streaming down its face, her insides grew cold and hollow and her legs began to tremble. This could only mean the worst. And what was the worst? She could not turn her mind toward the worst. Running home to Eng, she told him about the weeping Buddha and he held her in his arms.

"We are good people. We have done nothing wrong," he said.

"The Buddha is weeping, Eng. Do you not understand? Buddha is weeping!"

"Yes, I've heard. But there is nothing for us to do but wait. To wait and believe that we will be protected. Buddha is nothing if not patient. We, too, must be patient."

That evening Ona and Eng stood on their porch speaking with some neighbors. Most people now felt the future would be dark. All agreed the weeping Buddha was a foreboding omen. One neighbor said he and his family were leaving for Thailand that night and asked Eng and Ona to accompany them. Unlike his neighbor, Eng knew no one in Thailand and graciously refused the offer. Later when alone with her husband, Ona rebuked Eng for his refusal.

"We should go," she insisted. "They have already closed the temples and the schools. Things are going to get worse."

"Ona, we cannot go to Thailand. We have very little money and know no one there."

"Perhaps Lee's relatives can make room for us until we get work."

Eng sighed impatiently. His right eye twitched. "Ona! It's five with the children, seven with your parents. That's more than a little room. We cannot impose on our neighbor in this manner."

"But Lee offered for us to come," she pleaded, her hands trembling.

He shook his head. "He offered the journey only. And what shall we do once we arrive in Thailand? Live in the street? Here we have a home, food, work. People say the soldiers will not stay long. Lon Nol is not yet finished, and Pol Pot still has much work to do. His limited forces are already spread thin as the high clouds. Svay Sisophon is a stop along the way. They'll take our guns, some food and money, and then they'll be gone."

Tears filled her eyes, yet she addressed him in a formal tone. "None of the signs are good, husband. You know this. You should find a way for us to escape to Thailand."

Eng's face reddened. "It is far more dangerous for us to make a run for Thailand than to stand strongly among others."

"You make excuses because you're afraid to leave."

Eng took a step toward her and made a bitter face. "I am not afraid. You are afraid. Educated as you are, you are ready to take flight at the first omen. Remember, when you run, the tiger runs faster. It's better to stay still. We will stay here and only take flight if there is good cause."

Ona sat with her hands folded in her lap. She closed her eyes and let the tears run down her cheeks, feeling an irresistible sadness.

Eng's face softened and he leaned down, touching her lightly on the wrist. "You shame me with your reproach. I will protect you and the children. Of what are you afraid?"

Ona looked at him but said nothing. Eng felt great anguish at the sight of her beautiful face so wet with tears. He had never seen this before. His heart was stung with shame. He sat next to her and took her hand in his.

"Ona. If you truly want me to ask Lee to take us to Thailand, I will, though I think it is unwise. We'll go tonight."

"You really believe it is unnecessary to go?"

Stroking her wrist, he said, "Let's see what happens here. It's too soon to run. We have a life here and none in Thailand. If we are to start over a third time, under the worst conditions, first let's be sure we must."

"I have another idea," she said. "At least let's ask Ding-Toy if he'll take my parents and go with Lee to Thailand and send for us once they are established. We can send for my brother and his family as well. I'm very worried about him. I worry, too, about your brother. I wish we had some way to contact them."

Eng closed his eyes, his lips pursed in concentration. Finally he nodded. "My brother is in Battambang. I'm not too concerned about him. He can slip into Thailand in a few hours. I'll speak to Lee about your parents. But Ding may not want to leave us."

"We'll talk to him. He'll do as we ask."

The next morning when Ona and her husband arrived in the marketplace they found it entirely abandoned. They stood in the center of the street and stared into the emptiness. A gust of wind kicked up some dust and a lone dog barked somewhere. White birds wheeled above the river, their bright tiny eyes alert for food. The couple decided that someone must have told the vendors not to open their stalls. Ona and Eng quickly returned home and stayed inside all day.

That night Ona spoke to Ding-Toy about going to Thailand with his grandparents and Lee's family.

He looked at her and shook his young head, his long black hair covering his dark almond-shaped eyes for a moment. "No, Ma. I won't go."

"You must do as we ask, Ding. Grandma and Grandpa are old. They are nervous and I want them taken from here."

"Then we all go."

"We cannot all go. You know this and you know why. It's better for the family to be separated right now." She hesitated, searching for her words carefully. "To be more… spread out."

His gaze searched her face. "So, you fear the worst?"

She shook her head, trying to put on a face making light of the situation. "Father doesn't think things will be too bad. Still it's better to be wise. Your grandparents are old and need to be protected. And splitting up right now is a good idea."

Ding looked at her for a long time, as if he were going to argue further. But then he closed his eyes against the deep wave of sorrow washing over him, and he hung his head.

"You have to do this, Ding-Toy. You have to do it for all of us," his mother said.

~

Ding-Toy left with his grandparents, and the dry season settled over Svay Sisophon like a pall. Even the birds circling the river appeared listless. The blue sky faded with the heat and dryness and the slightest movement along the roads stirred up clouds of dust. Some people tried to leave the province at night, a few of their precious possessions tied in bundles with colorful rags, but they were turned back by the soldiers. The easy smiles and cheerful encouragement of the soldiers had gradually given way to a glum solemnity. Ona knew the soldiers were preparing for a different relationship with the people. Every day the commanding officer called a meeting in the long house with another group of soldiers. The people wondered why the officer never came out of his quarters. They often asked, "What does he do in there, day and night? Why doesn't he show us his face?"

It took several weeks to collect all the weapons and ammunition, which were then dumped into a huge pile in the center of the still-deserted marketplace. Once the roundup was over, the entire cache of arms was loaded into a truck and taken away and all pretense of friendliness on the part of the soldiers was completely abandoned. Now they became terse and even angry, talking to the people in curt, sarcastic tones.

An arrogant military voice booming over a loud-speaker called the people to a meeting in the marketplace. As they gathered, several trucks pulled in filled with people from neighboring provinces. When Ona saw her brother and his family among them she nearly swooned with joy.

"Why are they gathering everyone up?" she asked Eng.

He shrugged his shoulders, but his lips were drawn tightly and his face went pale. Seeing this she began to worry more. She dared not call to her brother for fear of provoking unwanted attention. He was in front and had not seen her, and she called to him with her mind—a childish thing, but she could not help it.

"Look," she said. "Do you see Ket and his family?"

Eng gave a slight nod and whispered, "Maybe we can get to them after the meeting."

Her brother sat with his wife and three children on the ground a few yards in front of Ona and her family. She calmed herself with the thought that after the meeting she and her family would make their way to him in the milling crowd and they would find a few moments to speak, reassuring each other and exchanging small but satisfying messages of care and consolation.

The soldiers stood in the shade of a canopy strung between the beds of two trucks while the people sat on the ground, many wearing colorful scarves and palm hats, some taking refuge from the heat beneath black umbrellas. Ona looked away from the backs of the loved ones she could not reach. She took in the people's worried faces, the shadows hiding in the eyes of the soldiers, while all around the insect sounds rose and fell in the dry, hot April air.

Placing her hand next to Eng's, she extended her pinkie so it touched his wrist. Now there was a bridge between them. She looked at her frightened daughters and forced a smile. Kunthea was nine and Tevy would celebrate her twelfth birthday in two months. Ona hoped by that time the tension in the province would be lifted and the family might enjoy a celebration. Perhaps she and her brother's family might even be together again.

A stern-faced soldier with a megaphone stood on the back of a truck. "All those who are doctors, teachers, soldiers, or policemen sit at the front with your families. The rest of the people sit in the back. You are all needed by your country. It must be rebuilt. We must plant and harvest rice, build bridges and roads, work in the fields, educate people, protect the nation, forge ahead for independence and national strength. Women, get rid of your jewelry and fancy clothes. No bright colors. There is serious work to be done. The good of the many must come before the good of the few. You will learn revolutionary songs. Every day there will be an educational session. Pol Pot leads the country now."

A few of her neighbors who had no education tried to pass themselves off as important. They were tricycle taxi drivers, farmers, and laborers who had purchased shirts from Lon Nol's soldiers as they fled. Her husband had no hope of impersonating an educated man, and when her brother and his family moved to the front, she swallowed dryly against a pang rising in her throat. She wanted to be close to her brother but would not leave her husband's side. They took their places at the back with the fish sellers and farmers.

The soldier explained that everyone must leave the village for a while so a final search for weapons could be made. He told the people in the back that they must work the fields to restore the country. He ordered those people to leave the meeting while soldiers began forming the others into ranks. The soldier said the people remaining behind would be taken to another part of the province to work.

"You are all needed by Pol Pot!" the soldier shouted. "Each to his own task. Quickly now, there is much work to do."

"Eng," she whispered, "we are being forced out. And they're keeping my brother and his family here. Why are they doing this?"

"He is among the professionals, Ona. I think he is safe. They need him to rebuild."

"And what of us?"

"I don't know, Ona. But I'm sure we are also needed."

"I'm frightened."

"We have done nothing wrong, Ona. There is nothing to fear." But the tremor in his voice spoke otherwise. Gathering their daughters near, he warned them to stay close.

Ona looked again for her brother, but already a line of stone-faced young soldiers had placed themselves between the people in the front and those who were already leaving. She hoped he would see her as she left with the crowd. She tried to look past the soldiers but their bodies and their rifles formed a wall.

Ona and Eng were allowed to load some clothes, several photographs, pots and pans, a lantern, a few small bags of rice, and blankets and pillows into the wagon Eng had built for their market wares. Then they put their daughters next to each other on the long bench crossing the wagon sides and they departed, pulling the wagon behind them. Ona's stomach ached as she considered their future, which now seemed so uncertain. They were forced to join a group heading east, accompanied by soldiers. The heat was intense and the road burned her feet through her sandals. At least the children had the wagon.

A half mile out of Svay Sisophon, she saw corpses rotting in the ditches on the side of the road. The sight of all those dead bodies heightened her sense of unreality. How quickly everything was worsening. She turned to her kids and told them to keep their eyes closed. But both girls had already hidden their faces in their hands. The sight of her children stricken with terror saddened and sickened her. They huddled together, staring fearfully into the dark of their cupped hands. Overhead the well-fed scavenger birds circled casually like fat diplomats at a banquet. The west wind swept the stench of decay over the crowds of people being driven past the fields.

Soldiers stationed to herd the crowd forward permitted families to leave the throng for a little while to cook a small pot of rice, which had to be quickly eaten before resuming the march under the blaring sun. Stealing quick glances behind her, Ona saw that the line of walking people was very, very long; thousands were being forced from their homes. More soldiers joined the line as it grew.

Occasionally someone recognized a face and word quickly spread through the crowd of people.

"Look! He used to be the head of the bank."

Or, "Hey! That's Suk Min, isn't it? He was a general for Lon Nol."

Some of the dead were missing fingers or ears or eyes. Many bodies had deep gouges made by bayonets. Some even had strips of skin missing. They had been flayed alive. Ona and Eng hardly looked at each other as they walked, but Ona was shocked to awaken to an old but profound truth hidden in the back room of her heart: a very important person with many decorations could be quickly transformed into a fly-covered corpse when the winds of fate shifted.

Eng whispered, "It looks like the new rulers will be worse than the old ones. They say they're for the people but they're all the same. They change one death mask for another."

Ona was so numb with fear she could hardly feel her feet upon the road. She wanted to answer her husband but could not. Eng frowned. "Ona, I was wrong. I have put you and the kids in great danger. We should have left for Thailand."

She cast a furtive glance in his direction. She needed him to be strong now, not guilty and discouraged. "Who knows what the best thing was, husband?" she whispered, trying to sound reassuring. "We need to be strong now. We need to remember our love."

Several yards ahead a soldier stepped into the line of people and pushed a man who was wearing glasses. "You're walking too slow! Move it."

The man snapped, "Why do you push me? I'm walking no slower than anyone else."

The soldier pushed the man down to the ground. His wife began to plead for her husband, but the soldier slapped her. When the man tried to help his wife, two other soldiers tore him from the line and shouted that everyone should keep moving.

The woman kept turning around as she walked ahead, waving her hands, calling to her husband, weeping.

When Ona passed the poor man, he was arguing with the three soldiers, protesting their treatment and asking that he be allowed to rejoin the line. Ona did not look at the man or the soldiers. After a few moments the crack of a rifle sounded behind her and she winced. The man's wife, still walking in front, began to wail.

Ona recalled the words of Bo, the monk. "Ona, now you must learn to be deaf and dumb and teach the children to do likewise. Learn silence and teach it to your kids."

Very softly, in nearly a whisper, Ona sang a poem she remembered from her childhood:

> *This morning the bright sun*
> *warmed my smiling face and*
> *many fish gathered in the net.*
> *Tonight there is no moon and*
> *I haven't a match for the candle.*

The poem struck her with a sense of profound and bitter irony. Never before had she understood it as she did at this moment.

She recalled Bo's words about life being like a dream. Though she felt permeated by a sense of unreality, the fearful expressions on the faces of her kids, the fear burning in her belly, the searing heat of the sun, and the long weary line of exiled people was anything but a dream. She recalled his assurance that she was consecrated. Was this consecration? Surely not. Then she remembered him putting his forefinger to his lips in a gesture of silence. That would be her consolation. She pressed that image against her heart like a seal. That would be the guiding image from now on for her, for her family, and probably for most everyone in Cambodia.

Occasionally a car passed slowly with suitcases tied to the roof, the wide frightened eyes of a child peering out the back window.

Ona and Eng were careful not to look into the eyes of any soldiers that they passed. More than once a soldier removed from the line either a straggler or a person who showed the slightest traces of annoyance when harassed. Soon after a rifle shot would crack in the distance. Ona and Eng never dared turn around to look.

I Have Done Nothing Wrong. What Should I Fear?

After three days of walking in the torturous heat, Ona and her family arrived exhausted at a large village far from the main road. The thick forest was bordered by small rice farms and burnt flatland. No river ran nearby and the rotten smell of decay floated in the thick, hot air. Eng found a shed full of cracks on the border of a field. They stayed for two nights in the shed, carefully rationing their food. How would they eat when it ran out? Thousands of people were now being led to the villages from the cities, driven into the fields to work for Pol Pot and the new revolutionary state. Word quickly spread that those who refused to leave their homes were summarily executed.

On the evening of the third day, a soldier banged

against the side of the shack with the butt of a rifle and told Eng he'd have to move his family closer to the center of the village. When he saw their daughters, he spoke gruffly. "Why do those girls have long hair? It's not sanitary. All of it will have to come off."

When the children immediately agreed and pleaded with the soldier not to harm them or their parents, calling him sir, he addressed them as Met Srei (Comrade Girls) and warned them not to use city language anymore and to speak like peasants. "No one gets special treatment anymore. You do not belong to your parents nor they to you. You all belong to Pol Pot now. If you work hard, you will become worthy of being true daughters of Pol Pot."

The family took up residence in another weathered, ramshackle shed on the grounds of a defunct mill. Each day more people led by soldiers streamed into the village.

One morning, two soldiers came to Eng and Ona's door and took their daughters roughly by their arms saying all children would now take up residence in The Little Children's Labor Camp on the other side of the village. The girls extended their arms in a pleading gesture and tearfully called to their parents. Ona fell to her knees and stuffed her fingers into her mouth to keep from screaming. Eng began to plead for his daughters, asking why they had to live in the children's camp.

The smaller of the soldiers answered, "Stop your begging, you silly fool, or I will bury a pick axe in your skull. Don't show any emotion. Show only fervor to work for the state. The children have their work to do and you have yours."

"At least leave the older one with us. Her name is Tevy. She is sickly, she has always been sickly," Eng said in as neutral a tone as he could muster.

The soldier sneered at him. "Work is an excellent cure for all illnesses. You have pampered her too much. Your weak family will be strengthened by rebuilding the state. You'd better rid yourself of your bourgeois ways and quickly."

Watching his children fade from view, Eng held his weeping wife and cursed himself for not fleeing with his family to Thailand when he had the chance.

Though the camp was close enough to the shed so Ona and Eng could see their daughters at the beginning and the end of the day, the children were allowed no visitors. Nor could they stay with their parents on any night. The soldiers told the people family visits might be allowed after a period of re-education for everyone.

Ona thought of her son every day. A curious memory returned to her, of a bad dream he had when he was very young. He had come blubbering to her bed and it took some time to understand what he was saying. He told her he had dreamt he was sitting at a little desk with blue paper and crayons, but all around him lay darkness. But it wasn't an ordinary darkness. The dark was simply nothing. A tiny light shone on the blue paper. He tried to draw a large crane that would carry him away on her back from this nothingness, but all he could draw was himself sitting at the desk.

She hadn't thought about young Ding's strange dream for years. Why did she recall it so vividly now? There were so many other things to remember about her strong son. How much he was like his Uncle Ket. How quickly he worked. How smart he was. How he could climb trees like a monkey and run like a fire on a trail of gasoline. And yet that defeating dream is what she recalled now. Was it an omen? She could not bear the thought that Ding-Toy had not made it to Thailand. Surely he had. Surely he and her parents were safe.

∼

There were many "jobs" to be done in and around the village. The children were often sent on a two- or three-day journey from the village to build roads. They worked twelve to fourteen hours together with a small meal break, their work involving pushing mud from one area to another and digging small rutted canals on either side of the road for drainage. Of course, with the first heavy rain the road would be completely washed out and the children would be blamed for poor workmanship. Rice was planted too, with no consideration for the seasons, and while it grew, it had to be constantly weeded. Rocks were moved from one place to another for no apparent reason. Grass was cut and burned for no purpose, and the people performed many other senseless tasks.

Everyone wondered at first why they were made to engage in so much useless activity. Was some great plan afoot that they were too naive to recognize? Was this part of the re-education plan for the people? Had the demons found their way into the bodies of their leaders? Had Pol Pot gone mad? One answer seemed as good as another, and after a while the people no longer questioned, even to themselves. Baskets were woven and large trenches were dug in the forest. The soldiers—or yotears, as they were called—told the people that coconut trees would be planted in the trenches, which again made no sense, since wild coconuts already grew in the forest. No one realized until later that the trenches would actually be useful to bury great mounds of corpses when starvation and execution became rampant.

A bell sounding at the center of the village awoke Ona and Eng each morning, long before the dawn. Holding a large palm leaf in hand like a plate, they were given break-fast—a small portion of rice served from a huge iron pot. Then they were assigned to a work crew, carrying dirt and rocks from one field to another. A soldier would stake out a piece of ground, and that would mean all the rocks in the area would have to be removed by the end of the day. If the work was not completed, more work would be given the next day. The people used dull, rusted shovels with splintered handles that cut and blistered their hands. Dual buckets hung across a long pole draped across the shoulders were used to transport the rocks.

Of course the cleared fields were left fallow, and frequently the rocks were returned in big piles to the fields from which they had been previously removed. The combination of such heavy meaningless work given with so little food quickly wore away the bodies and minds of the people, and the need to survive under desperate conditions expressed itself in ugly ways. Collaborators, called mekongs, monitored work and reported anyone who moved too slowly or grumbled or was suspected of plotting against the new order. Corrective action was swift: pointless interrogation followed by a beating with rifle butts or pick axes until "the criminal of the state" was dead. "Bad" children were sometimes given the "plastic bag." This entailed tying a child's hands behind the back and taping a plastic bag over the head until death occurred by asphyxiation.

A mekong reported one of Ona's neighbors as an enemy of Pol Pot because he complained about the lack of food. He was dragged to the center of the village before the evening meal was distributed. Before the horrified eyes of the inmates of the camp, including the children, he was stripped naked and ridiculed by the soldiers who pushed him to his knees. "Plead for your life," they shouted, "and perhaps Pol Pot will forgive you. Come on, plead for your life!" The man clasped his hands in front of his face and said, "Please don't kill me. I have children. I am a good man. I did not complain. I will work very hard." Many in the crowd looked down because they did not want to see the man killed. Ona saw her children gathered with the other kids behind the fence that enclosed The Little Children's Labor Camp. She wanted to shout for them to cover their eyes but dared not.

The soldier holding the pistol in the man's face nodded and smiled. "Okay, okay. Get up then and get your food." The crowd breathed a sigh of relief, and as the man rose, the soldier quickly lowered the gun again and blew the man's face off, scattering bone and teeth in the bloody dirt.

Ona's knees buckled. Eng held her to prevent collapse. "Don't look," he whispered. "Keep your eyes shut."

But it was too late. Everyone had looked up once they thought the man was saved. And so everyone had seen. And that is exactly what the soldiers wanted.

Staggering away from the execution, her mind reeling, Ona fell to her knees and looked at the sky. A red bird sailed over some tree tops in the distance, free from the horror that held her family captive. No sight that she might see, no sound that she might hear, no surface that she might touch would bring relief to her anguished heart. She saw her kids through chicken wire, their eyes wide with fear and hunger, their hearts longing to return to their parents. She could hear in her husband's voice his guilt and helplessness. When she touched her cooking pot, she felt its emptiness, an emptiness so cold in spite of the heat. The world had grown the skin of a demon with an iron hide. Her family had fallen into an unspeakable hell.

The red bird disappeared from view. Life as she had known it was over forever. She would never go back to the plantation. She would never return to Svay Sisophon. She would never sit with carefree ease among her family. Even if the camp life ended right now and she could return home safely with her family, she could never go back to being the Ona she was. That Ona had died with the man she saw killed. Though nothing could explain what was happening to her family and neighbors, to pretend that things might be different was foolish and even dangerous. Things could not be different. They were the way they were. Facing her now was an abyss without measure, a darkness filled with flying knives. She uttered a fervent prayer to the gods to protect her, her children and her husband, her brother and his family, her parents. But no feeling of any promise existed at the end of her prayers. Silence followed, a silence that did not listen, only waited. For her thoughts, for her tears.

There was only empty sky above her and the rocky ground on which she walked.

$\sim$

One day while clearing rocks in the field, Ona noticed that everything had become extremely quiet. Looking around she saw the supervising soldier sleeping under a tree. Every few moments flies landed on his face and he brushed at them. She hoped the flies would not awaken him. A few other prisoners were also clearing rocks on the other side of the field. They moved slowly under the weight of their hunger-ridden fatigue and perpetual fear, like figures from a nightmare. She paused to take a breather, glad to be free for a few moments of the merciless watch of the soldier. Even without the slow starvation, the relentless surveillance of the soldiers and their spies was unbearable. To be watched continually by angry and treacherous eyes drained one's inner life. It was like being invaded from within. She could find no solace anywhere, even within herself. They lived inside as well as outside—watching and waiting for the prisoners to do something wrong so they could torture or kill them. It was like being turned inside-out. And now in this moment allowing reflection, Ona's teeth chattered despite the heat. What should she think now that she had a moment to think? She found herself alone with herself and at the same time turned against herself.

Furtively she looked around for something familiar, something to give her some small comfort. Heat shimmered off the palm trees and even the stirring of the wind brought more heat. It felt as if she were submerged in a steaming soup of heat. The sleeping soldier, the midday heat, the poor creatures clearing rocks, the swarming flies and insects, and most of all the terrible silence that she heard over the sounds of the day, filled her with a dread so profound that she could hardly breathe. The silence was death calling to her:

Ona, Ona. Your life is for naught. Everything you have ever known and loved has been merely a variation of my form. It is and has always been only I who await you. Perish and be gone.

Someone was walking her way, a man dressed in a

filthy, tattered white shirt and baggy green trousers. His gait seemed familiar. He raised his hand very slightly in greeting. Something about that movement also struck her as familiar. He drew closer. Ket! She glanced back at the soldier still sleeping and stepped toward her brother.

"Ona, my beloved sister…" He tentatively reached to embrace her but pulled back when he saw the sleeping soldier.

She was so happy she began to cry. "What are you doing here?" she asked, reaching her hands out. He looked thin and frail, already aged, his clothes tattered in thin strips that hung from his gaunt arms.

He reached out his fingers to her. She raised her arm. Their hands were no more than a foot apart. "I'm with a transient crew. They decided to send me to work here for a while. I'm clearing rocks."

She nodded. "I'm carrying rocks and dirt from the fields to the mountain."

He looked so weak but still proud, more alert than most. So much she wanted to say. More than that, she wanted to embrace him.

He glanced again at the soldier. "We're all so hungry. "The yotears are starving us. You look so thin."

She took a tiny wobbly step forward. "And you, you look like a scarecrow. How is Shon-Li? The kids?"

"Very hungry, tired and frightened, but still well. We dream of food all the time. The children wake up crying because they are so hungry. They want to go back to sleep because at least in their dreams, they eat."

Her eyes filled with tears. "Your children are with you?"

"Yes. Why?"

"Kunthea and Tevy are in a labor camp with all the other children."

He put his hand to his head, as if to shield his eyes. "I'm so sorry, dear sister. I'm sorry about all of this," he said, sweeping his arm around to indicate the hot wasteland surrounding them. What about our parents? What about Ding-Toy?"

"We sent them to Thailand when it started. I believe they're safe. I miss them terribly."

He nodded. "I find the hunger makes it hard to think. Hard to feel even."

She moved another inch closer to him. She whispered, "I am always dreaming of food. My nights turn around salted fish with *prahoc,* kepi, rice cakes. I dream that Shon-Li and I are making *am sam chruk* again. Do you recall that delicious meal we had when we were last gathered together?" She didn't care about the soldier anymore. She reached out and Ket took her in his thin arms. She could feel the bones pressing through his thin flesh. They both cried softly.

"Yes, how can I forget, dear sister? What's the matter with your eyes? Why are they so red? Have you been crying much?"

She would not let him go. "Not so much anymore. The baskets are heavy and sometimes I get dirt in my eyes. I squeeze betel juice into them to help. I notice they're becoming a little blurry."

Gently he pulled away and looked intently into her eyes. "You know, Shon complains of the same thing. She said many women and the girls in the village have the same problem. Blurry eyes."

"It's the dirt we carry. It gets in our eyes."

"The men carry dirt too. It doesn't have quite the same effect. A few complain about it. But no one wears glasses anymore. The yotears say wearing glasses means you're an intellectual and more possibly an enemy of the state. They hate anything intellectual. They hate thought itself."

Ona nodded and glanced nervously around her. Thankfully, the soldier was still asleep. "How long have you been at this camp?"

"Not long. A couple of weeks. They've been moving us around quite a lot. They know I was a constable. They're sending me and Shon and the kids to another province. A group is leaving tomorrow. I'll be given a good job."

"Are you sure?"

"Yes, yes. It'll be good."

She looked into her brother's weary eyes. "Ket. Don't go with them. Run away to Thailand. Do it tonight."

He winced, then looked away. "Stop it, Ona. So long as we do what we're told, our chances are good. They know I'm skilled and can help the new regime. Nothing will happen to us. Anyway, how can we escape to Thailand with the kids? We'll be shot. It's too late to escape."

She clasped her hands before her, praying to him. "Escape by yourself. We'll look after Shon-Li and the kids."

He stepped back and his voice broke. "Ona, I have done nothing wrong. What should I fear?"

"You should fear for your life and the lives of your loved ones," she answered. "In your heart you already know that. We all do. It doesn't matter how good any of us has been. It doesn't matter. We're like fish in a net."

Ket shook his head, but then his eyes turned kind and gentle. He stepped forward and touched his sister's bony shoulder reassuringly. "I am very careful with the soldiers. I praise Pol Pot, the dirty bastard. We keep our mouths shut. I am blameless. Why would they kill us? But they would certainly harm Shon-Li and the kids if I ran."

What he said was both true and false. He must know that the soldiers had already killed careful, blameless people, so why not he and his family? On the other hand, if her brother and his family ran, they certainly would be killed. What could she say? Reaching to embrace him again, she felt as if she were thrusting her hands through the bars of a cage.

"Oh, I have missed you so much, Ket. Why has this terrible thing happened to us?"

Hugging her, he whispered, "What can I say, Ona? How can I know? I'm in the dark like you and everyone else. It is the time of the enemy. We have to hang on until the storm passes." He scratched his chin and looked into the dust. It almost looked as if he were smiling. "Do you know what my little one said?"

"Koy? How is my little angel boy?"

"He is an amazing child, Ona. I believe he has your gifts. Like you he is filled with love and vision. Last night he told his mother that he saw a herd of tiny winged horses gather round his mat. They told him not to be afraid of anything." Ket's voice cracked. "He grasped his mother's hand and said he would not let go until she stopped being afraid too."

She looked away from Ket's face because she did not want to sob.

"Look!" he exclaimed in a whisper, digging his hand into his pocket. "I have something to show you."

At the sight of what he held in his palm, new tears ran from her eyes. The shell she painted for him years before—the white goose still aloft beneath dark clouds. "Remember what you said to me?" he asked.

She wiped her burning eyes and nodded.

He chucked her gently beneath the chin, lifting her head until their eyes met. "It has brought me great strength during this terrible time. I believe it is enchanted, enchanted with the power of love. I keep it with me at all times. Tell me, do you think I am still strong and swift?"

She poked at the ribs beneath his rag shirt. "I think now you are skin and bones."

They laughed softly. Again she heard the terrible silence. In their laughter. In the trees. In the keening of the insects. "You will not take flight to Thailand?" she asked.

"Sister, please don't worry. We'll be okay."

She turned to look over her shoulder. The soldier sleeping beneath the tree was stirring. "Before you leave tomorrow, take our wagon," she said as Ket began to walk away, pocketing his shell and forcing a smile.

Early next day, Ket and his family left with the group for another province.

∼

That night she dreamt of being lost in the dense jungle lying beyond the borders of Svay Sisophon, calling for her mother and father. The shrill cries of the insects pierced her ears and the smell of dung was overpowering. Sweat poured from her face and soaked her clothes and she began to run crying through the thick foliage. In a clearing she came upon an enormous bridge, unlike any on earth. It was nearly as high as the clouds and made of thick, black, crisscrossed girders that gleamed meanly in the sun like the back of a gigantic dragon, wide enough to carry ten trucks side by side. At its entrance sat two large stone demons with red bodies and black faces, long barbed tongues protruding like spikes from their snarling mouths, bright with razor teeth. She couldn't imagine how high or long the bridge was, but it frightened her more than being lost in the jungle.

She awoke in a sweat and sat up in the darkness. Eng was breathing quietly next to her. She lit a candle and poured herself some water from an old pot that stood next to her mat. The cup shook in her hand and she braced herself with the other hand so she could better view the dark cracks in the old porcelain. When had that cup started to crack like that? It was the last one in a large set her mother had given her for her wedding. How much time had passed since she lay with Eng in their home by the river, looking at the beautiful yellow moon lazily drifting in the sky through their large bedroom window? In those days they had shared so much. Now between them they had one battered cup. How long before? How long to go?

~

Two days later the mekong Im from Ona's work group called her from her detail to speak to her. Taking her aside she said, "Your brother was here on a detail. Someone in the camp recognized him. Two days ago he and his family left with some soldiers. I followed them a little into the forest. I climbed a tree to keep them in view…"

Ona began to sway, and moaning, she leaned against the woman, who shoved her, saying, "Stand up! Don't be a fool. Listen to me. The youngest child called for water and when your sister-in-law drew some water from a ditch one of the soldiers began to beat her. Your brother jumped between his wife and the soldier and two other soldiers began to beat the two of them with their rifles."

The woman paused, looking carefully into Ona's face, her eyes burning with curiosity. "Your brother kneeled before the soldiers, saying, 'We are blameless, we are innocent, we are good people. Please do not kill us.' The soldiers killed the youngest first, swinging him by his ankles and bashing his head against a tree. Then they shot the rest of the family. One after another. They were all together.

Your brother died last."

Ona looked into the woman's face, now a dark blur. "You're lying," she said. "That did not happen. The soldiers told you to test me. This is a test," she said, grabbing hold of the woman's arm.

The woman began pulling her along saying, "Come with me, I'll show you your test!"

The mekong took Ona into a clearing where some packages of rice lay with the label she knew her brother to favor. Beside the packages of rice were piles of adults' and children's clothes, familiar and covered in thick black blood. Then the leader pointed to a tree with dried blood and gore splattered over the trunk. Ona wanted to cry out but couldn't. She put her hand inside her shirt and stroked her racing heart. Then her knees gave way and her vision grew dark and blurry.

The mekong walked Ona back to the detail and told her to pick up her tools, but Ona could hardly see or move her arms. "Ona," the leader admonished, "you'd better work hard."

Ona swayed. She wanted to die, but she was still living. "I have no strength," she pleaded.

"Ona! You'd better find the strength! The soldiers are watching you to see if you show any signs of anger or sorrow. If you do, they will kill you. Or they might kill your kids first."

"How can I not feel anger or sorrow?" Ona sobbed. "They've killed my brother and his entire family. I am not made of clay."

"It doesn't matter," the woman said with bitter vehemence. "It doesn't matter who they kill. And it doesn't matter what you're made of. Clay. Flesh. Shit! It doesn't matter. Those who remain alive cannot show remorse. If you show remorse, your family and you will die just like your brother and his family. They told me to tell you all this in more detail, but I spared you. I'm sure you've seen enough to imagine for yourself. I'm to tell them your reaction. But don't worry, I will not tell that you cried out."

Ona gaped at the leader and tried to speak. Her mouth worked but no sounds would come. Through the blur, Ona saw two pinpoints of reflected light, the woman's eyes, cold and eerie like the eyes of a crow.

The woman's voice was low and raspy. "Ona. I should tell them how you're behaving. Stop it now. If you show any sign that your loyalty goes to your brother and not Pol Pot they will kill you. That is certain. Don't be a fool." She handed Ona a rusted hand shovel. "Your brother is lost. Why leap into the void after him? Here. Take this and get to work."

Ona could not see. Everything she looked at was

blurry and wavering, as if she were seeing the world from the bottom of a shallow pond.

In the days following, she kept a frozen smile on her face and uttered a choked laugh when anyone spoke to her, so as not to endanger herself and her family. But at night in her shack she crawled beneath her filthy blanket and sobbed. Her husband clutched her hand and warned her when he thought soldiers were approaching. Her vision remained dim except when she dealt with some especially terrifying situation; then it would become a blurred brightness, like a concentration of stars or clustering pinpoints of sunlight on water.

She fell ill with a fever that lasted for weeks and kept her immobilized on the floor of her shack. The soldiers examined her and told her she was faking. At first she was frightened of what they might do, but then in her delirium she began to welcome death. Only the corpse was beyond the torments of the yotears and the mekongs.

During her feverish days and nights of illness, she was tormented by terrible images and would awaken to realize that nothing she dreamt or might possibly dream could be worse than the reality of the camp. At these times she would return to sleep and pray never to wake.

Again and again she dreamt of the black bridge, guarded by its barb-tongued demons, its black steel gleaming in the sun like the back of a gigantic dragon. It rose above the earth, arching over an immense ocean and disappearing in the clouds. Hot wind blew on her face and the keening scream of insects pierced her ears. She could not see nor imagine where the bridge ended. She found herself walking on the bridge, quite near its center, the ocean below stretched out for as far as she could see. An ocean like this was impossible; surely it covered the entire world with its bottomless depths. She saw her brother walking toward her, naked, his face and body black. He called her name and beckoned for her to come near, but his appearance terrified her.

He extended his hand. "Ona, come, come with me."

"Where do you live now?"

"I live in a province on the other side," he said, looking back over his bony shoulder.

"Is it good there?"

"Yes, it is very good. There is plenty to eat and a lovely river."

"Do you have work?"

"Yes, but not like before. I make paper lanterns. We place poems inside them and float them on the river."

She woke Eng and told him about the dream, but he was not sure what it meant—whether her brother was telling of better times to come or that he was beckoning her toward the grave. Eng held Ona in his arms and asked her not to die. "He is gone," she cried. "His family is gone. Pol Pot has taken away our lives and yet we still live."

Crying, he held her in his arms and rocked her back and forth, terrible guilt stabbing him over what had befallen his family, feeling helpless, stifled, doomed. How he wished he could speak to his brother about the thoughts that plagued his mind in the late hours of the night. Why didn't he take the chance and flee with the family to Thailand? Ona had been right from the start. He had been afraid to leave. But there was something else. Remembering that first day when the soldiers had come into the village shouting praise for the revolution, his first clear thought had been to take his family and run as fast as a typhoon moves across the sea. But he shunned that voice that spoke within him, that deep voice of truth, and clung to the childish hope that the soldiers would be good. He knew they were devil pigs the moment he saw them, their phony smiles showing white fangs, their eyes narrowed with suppressed malice. He had sniffed the madness in the air but ignored it, because at the moment it had been more comfortable to stay where they were than to flee.

At least Ding-Toy escaped to Thailand with her parents. Often he and Ona spoke of them. She prayed for Ding every day. How they both missed their precious boy.

Neither would believe he was dead. Surely he was thriving in Thailand with her parents, awaiting reunion with his parents and sisters.

Then he would think again about his reluctance to flee. *No, I really didn't know what was going on. Looking back on it in the light of what I now know, it seems I shirked my responsibility to make the best decision for my family. But I didn't know, I really didn't know.*

Back and forth these thoughts would go, like two malicious children on a seesaw, and even though he was exhausted from his useless work of carrying sand and rocks and sticks, many nights his thoughts awakened him. He would lie on his mat, his body half dead, his mind numb with dread and guilt, and wish that the soldiers would kill him.

~

Gradually Ona recovered, but she was too weak to work in the fields, so she was assigned to care for two young children, a boy and a girl belonging to the commanding officer in charge of the village. At first she thought she'd hate the kids because they were healthy and clean and well fed, while most of the kids in The Little Children's Labor Camp, except those belonging to the mekongs, were starving to death like their parents. On the contrary, Ona felt glad that the officer's children did not have to endure hunger and terror like the others. They were only children after all, innocent of the hell that surrounded them. Like any other children, they wanted to play and hear stories. Like any kids, they craved food, love, and diversion.

She was curious about what had happened to the mother of these well-fed children but didn't ask them because she might be killed for her curiosity. She was curious about the commander too. At times, intense curiosity seized her, and she welcomed it because it intercepted her hunger. She was even curious about her curiosity, which she considered to be mostly inane and irrelevant. Might it be just another form of her hunger, her curiosity? Maybe her hunger for food had become bored with itself and replaced itself with an urgency to know things that really didn't matter to her anymore.

What would happen next? Who would disappear from the camp at night? When would the rains come again? Could she safely hide a stolen berry in her ragged clothes? Was there any work done by the camp that had any real use? What did the officer look like? What did he do walled up in his hut all day? Why did he never show his face? Was he ashamed of what was being done to the people? Did he enjoy the brutal and stupid terror he inflicted through his soldiers? Did he know about all the killings that took place, the ones in the rice paddies, the ones in the forest beyond the camp? Had he ordered her brother's death?

As the weeks passed, the children responded to Ona's gentle sweetness with love, and they even slipped her bits of food. She shared some of the meager booty with her husband, but gave the greater share to her kids, whenever she might catch them for a moment in the evening by the fence enclosing the children's camp. She'd put on a brave smile for her daughters and they would smile weakly and wave goodbye like tired old ladies. Kunthea looked thinner and weaker than Tevy, the black circles so thick around her eyes that her face had the look of a starving raccoon. For a moment, hands touched and Ona would quickly slip a spoonful of rice rolled up in a leaf or a bite of bread through the fence, her heart longing to breech the fence and take her children into her arms. Then she would feel grateful that her eyesight was so bad. At least the misery etched into her daughters' faces was not so clearly seen. But this made the sound of their voices as they called "Ma, Ma" all the more painful to hear. Both children sounded so weak, so old. Eng rarely came to the fence with Ona. He could not bear to see his kids thin as grasshoppers. He'd wait at the hut for any news from Ona when she returned at sunset, her arms aching with emptiness.

Then she would see the commander's children with their shiny hair, bright eyes and plump cheeks, the ones she cared for while her own languished behind the wire. Sometimes she felt like strangling them. No, they were only children, after all, innocent as her own.

Ona finally worked up the courage to ask about their mother, but they did not know what happened to her. "One morning she wasn't there," the boy told her. "Our father said she ran into the forest. But I don't believe him."

"Why?" Ona asked.

The boy shrugged his shoulders and tears came into his deep-set eyes. "I don't believe him," he repeated.

As the days passed, everything viewed through Ona's eyes appeared to be dissolving. One evening while her husband was still working in the fields, she stood by the fence while the children looked for their parents for a few minutes before dark. She squinted and strained but could not discern any faces. The children gathering at the fence appeared to her in a blurry, moving cluster of dull color. They were fingers painfully squeezed together, faces barely a smudge. She turned her ear towards the fence hoping that her kids were there and would call to her.

She heard Kunthea's voice nearby. "Ma, Ma!"

She groped her way slowly toward the voice. "Kunthea?"

"I'm so hungry, Ma. Do you have anything for me?"

"No, my little heart. Not tonight. Where is your sister?"

"She's sick, Ma. She couldn't get up yesterday or today. Her poo is full of blood. The yotears have built a hospital hut, because the real hospital is too far away. She's in there. The mekongs look after her. My friend Mliss died last week. They have a big pit for all the kids in the forest. We can hardly do the work. They told us today that if we're not good and don't work hard for Pol Pot, we're going to get the plastic bag."

Ona knelt down and stroked her child's face through the fence but said nothing. Her voice had been stolen by anguish.

She decided not to tell her husband about Tevy because his condition also appeared to be deteriorating and she feared he blamed himself for his family's internment. But the thought of her being helpless while her daughter was sick was worse than her hunger and fear combined. She decided to beg the commanding officer of the camp for help.

Breathless with terror, she knocked upon his door while expecting to be dragged outside and shot for daring to approach him. A shrill voice called from behind the door. "Who is it?" Always they spoke in that voice, the soldiers, the mekongs, the leaders—that piercing voice of one stuck by thorns.

"It is I, the one who cares for Met Pich and Met Sovann," she called back, her voice low and meek. "I, your loyal comrade of the state and sister of Pol Pot, beg a word with you."

"Come in, then."

She opened the door, but a dark curtain was drawn across it. The man inside stepped back into the shadows of the hut. "What is it?" he asked, his gravely voice filled with irritation.

Ona got down on her knees and lowered her head, bowing it over and over as she spoke.

"Please forgive me, I am so sorry to annoy you," she repeated three times. "I have two children in The Little Children's Labor Camp. One of them—her name is Tevy—I hear is very ill. If I might be allowed to see her… If some medicine might be given…"

He emitted a long sigh. "Foolish, selfish woman. There is nothing I can do to help your child. Many children are sick. There is no medicine and little food for anyone. Here you are relieved of the labor of the fields, and still you ask for more favors. You work slowly and stumble about and pretend you are ill, and now you ask me for more help. Look at all you have been given already. Still you show no gratitude. Your greed sickens me. Get away from me now."

Leaving, she wept silently into her cupped hands, still hearing his voice accusing her of selfishness and greed. It was insane to say she was selfish and greedy. Yet, she felt insulted by his accusation. How odd that she still expected understanding or at least sanity from the yotears, the mekongs, the commanding officer. Then she realized this was because she still thought of everyone—prisoners, yotears, soldiers, commanders—as sharing a common world. She still assumed that the persecutors knew what they were doing was wrong. They knew good people were being destroyed in the name of crazy ideas. But now it occurred to her that perhaps they knew no such thing and indeed their reality was entirely different from her own. In their reality, she was selfish and greedy and lazy and expected special treatment. In their reality, they were providing a great service to Brother Number One. And yet all around them the innocent fell like fruit from a tree. The disparity between the two views made her mind reel.

∾

Every time Ona's eyesight began to improve, another friend, neighbor, or relative was killed and her semi-blindness returned. She heard no further word of her daughter. Her own illness returned. She finally told her husband about Tevy, begging him to get the girls and plan an escape with a friend who knew the jungle and had made up his mind to get to Thailand. But she knew even as she pleaded that it was futile. Eng, despite the scraps his wife smuggled, was in the later phases of starvation and too weak to run. Anyway, he would not leave Ona behind. Even if he could, trenches dug around the camp and filled with lethal dung-coated bamboo stakes cut to razor sharpness poked at the sky and waited to impale a daring prisoner. Some stakes could be seen and some not; the stakes in clear view were cleverly arranged so that when they were avoided they often caused the wary prisoner to fall into a hidden ditch and be impaled by others. The soldiers would let a victim, unlucky enough to survive the initial trap, writhe in agony until he or she died and then leave the rotting corpse where it fell as a reminder to all those who considered escape. Those who did escape could expect family members to be tortured and killed as retribution.

"We will die here together," Eng said to his wife. "I will not go on without you. Get well and we will plan our escape."

"It will be too late already. We will be too weak."

He shook his head. "No. Get well and we will escape."

"Why do you say that when you know it is not true?"

They were lying in their little shack at the edge of a

field. The night sky was filled with stars and a cooling wind blew through the cracked, ramshackle wooden slats. Through the window shone a sliver of new moon. She raised her hand and pointed to it. "Remember when the sight of that made us happy?"

"You see it?"

"My eyes can see tonight. The blindness comes and goes."

"It's still beautiful, is it not?"

She peered at it for a moment and said, "Yes, it is. How can it look down upon this and still shine so brightly?"

Eng slowly sat up next to his wife. "Because it can see a time when we will no longer have to endure Pol Pot."

"Do you really think so, Eng? Do you really think we are not doomed?"

He shook his head and his voice cracked. "I don't understand what has happened. Or why. That is worse than anything. Not knowing why this has happened to us. We are innocent. I feel it is my fault this has happened."

"You know better than that. Look at the many suffering all around us. How can you have anything to do with this? You have always done your best to take care of me and the kids. Stop thinking these evil thoughts. Think instead of a time when we may be free. But do you really think such a time will come?"

In a voice choked with tears, he answered, "Truly, I think not. And I cannot rid myself of the thought that this is my fault. Had I listened to you, we might be safe in Thailand by now. I know it is a bad thing to think and that it weakens me further, but I cannot help myself. My guilt covers me like…" He threw his hands up and shook them, his face reddening. "Like a second skin." He fell forward and wept.

"I want you to do me a favor," she said calmly, touching his arm. "Fetch our photographs."

"What do you want with the photos?"

"Please, do as I ask. I want to look at them one more time. Fetch them."

Eng continued to cry. He feared his wife would die soon. Lying on her filthy straw bed she looked like a pile of sticks beneath thin and tattered rags, skin yellow and dry as an old paper lantern, dark circles growing beneath her swollen and bloodshot eyes, her once beautiful hands curled claw-like at her sides. Surely those hands would never again work their magical skill with paints and a brush.

Turning over a rock in the corner of the shack, he dug the ground beneath with his hands, unearthing a small wooden box. In it were some pieces of jewelry, a small turquoise Buddha, two small golden candle holders, and a handful of photographs.

Eng placed the photos on her stomach like an offering. He moved with the tenderness that he had used when he first held his children, only now his hands shook and looked like those of a man in his eighties.

Ona went through the photos one by one, savoring each one, a small treasure of memory. She lingered most on a picture of herself and her brother standing side by side, his arm around her shoulder, an easy smile on his face. The picture had been taken a few months after her marriage, when the two families had taken a short vacation to the Great Lake, Tonle Sap. Ket wore a yellow shirt, two sizes too big for him, printed with large, silly flowers. His wife had purchased it for its sharp "American look." Yet even in his ridiculous shirt, he looked great, his smile so big and confident.

She held the photo so Eng could see it. "Remember?"

"Yes. The trip to Tonle Sap. How could I forget? You almost drowned there. I rescued you."

She gave him a weak smile. "I was fine. You thought you rescued me."

He smiled weakly. "Really? As I remember you looked desperate."

"Perhaps I was a little frightened. But I think you were

more frightened than me." She handed him the pictures. "Burn them," she said.

His eyes opened wide. "What? What are you saying?"

"Burn them. I am saying to burn them. They must be destroyed."

"Why?"

"We have to burn everything that reminds us of what we once had; we have to burn everything so that if we die, we die without regrets. You must shed your skin of guilt. We cannot dwell on what was."

"I do not wish to burn them, Ona. Please."

Ona began to sob. "My Tevy is already dying and I can do nothing. What then can I do for myself? Burn the pictures, Eng. Burn them."

He stared at her, his eyes spilling tears.

She shut her eyes and the lids trembled. For a long time she lay there, tears running down the side of her cheek, unable to speak.

Finally, she took a deep breath, opened her eyes, and stroked her husband's cheek until he looked into her eyes. "Burn them, husband," she said gently.

Eng took the photos and set them on fire.

"The fire is taking away the past," Ona said. "Everything we ever cherished has been ruined forever. We must accept this."

Eng shook his head weakly. "No, Ona, we have each other, we have the children. Tevy is not dead. We still have your parents."

"No, no," she answered, "we cannot hope for anything now. We must think of everything, even ourselves, as already gone."

Eng lowered his head and wept. That night as he slept, he cried and moaned in his sleep so loudly that Ona awoke and sat up on her mat. His body jerked on the mat as though he were getting electric shocks. He looked as if he were trying to run away from some terror in his dreams. His hands jerked in front of his face as if fending off blows. Extending her hand to shake his shoulder, she considered waking him from his nightmare, then rejected the idea. Why wake him from his nightmare? His reality was far worse than anything he could ever dream.

She lay back down and fell asleep, nourishing a secret wish to cross the black bridge at last.

Meetings on the Black Bridge

In a black dream on the black bridge Ona met her daughter Tevy.

"Ma, help me," the child said, extending her hand, so emaciated that the veins and bones were clearly visible.

Ona inched toward her daughter, her legs moving through a thick syrup. With each step she took, Tevy moved away an equal distance.

"Tevy. Don't move. I'm coming."

"Ma, it hurts. My stomach hurts." The child grabbed her belly and cried out. "It hurts! It hurts!"

Ona, still trying to reach her child, called out, "Tevy! Look at me, Tevy. Look!"

Tevy lifted her huge, bony head and looked at her mother. "Mom," she said, her eyes welling up in tears of blood. "Help me."

Ona woke with a cry and grabbed around in the darkness until she found a match. Lighting it, she glanced around the room and was relieved that her eyes weren't too bad tonight. The little flame appeared clear and distinct. Her vision came and went, ranging from nearly blind to very poor. But she could see moonlight spilling between the large gaps between the slats on the far wall and illuminating the mud floor in lines of white. She quietly crept out of the shack, glancing back over her shoulder, alert for the stirring of her husband's body. She had only taken a few steps on the path leading down the hill and toward the fence surrounding The Little Children's Labor Camp when she stumbled, lost her balance, and fell. Dizzy from hunger, weak from sickness, she slowly climbed to her feet, using a large stone for purchase, and stood again on wobbly legs. Each step on the short journey felt like a mile.

Alternately sweating and shivering, she crept forward on stick legs. Her body trembled like the broken wings of a bird. The half moon was bright, tilted like a bowl, spilling milky light against the rims of tall, black mountainous clouds. Its light illuminated the path and even the fence surrounding the camp. She continued to both shiver and perspire as she closed the distance with agonizing slowness. She would not even let the thought of being caught enter her mind, nor even the thought of what she would do once she reached the fence. Tevy had called her.

Halfway down the path she stumbled again and fell. She waited on the ground several minutes to catch her breath and pray that she would have the strength to get up and keep walking. Breathing the dark air, her ears alert for soldiers, she pictured Tevy's face in the dream, meeting on the black bridge, bloody tears rolling down her cheeks. Oddly, she drew strength from the image. If hope was lost, so was all burden except the final one: to meet the end with courage, eyes turned toward the gods in spite of everything.

Still, when she thought that Tevy might still be alive, that any or all of her family might escape the camp, she was terrified of the yotears and stricken with fear for her child. She felt, too, that perverse sense of curiosity as she managed to climb to her feet again. How did she manage it? Where did she find the strength to stand up again and walk? Was it life itself impelling her? The power of her spirit? Yes, that must be it. As a child she soared on the ecstatic wings of her spirit; and now her spirit drove her on from the depths of her agony.

The area around the fence had no trees or bushes and a yotear could easily see her, so she eased down and crawled slowly out of the brush, inching her way toward the fence.

Her arms and knees scraped against the ground as she moved and choked back the urge to cough. Panting heavily and very dizzy by the time she reached the edge of the compound, she thought of standing but decided to rest first.

How would she ever get over this fence? It would be difficult to stand up, let alone climb. And even if she could get over the fence, how would she find Tevy? She would have to go into each dark hut without waking anyone up. Impossible.

Finally grabbing hold of the wire and about to pull herself to a standing position, she heard something behind her. Her skin crawled with fear and she held her breath. Footsteps? She froze, face pressed into the dirt. The sound of footsteps stopped behind her. Was someone standing right behind her? She closed her eyes and waited. Torture then death. Or worse, they'd make her witness the execution of her family and then torture and kill her. Trembling, she pissed herself as she waited for the boot in her back, the pick axe in the skull, the sound of an evil voice telling her to stand. She awaited the unspeakable nothing of death—or the welcoming light of the gods. Who really knew?

For a long time she lay there waiting, listening to her gasping breath and watching her vision fade with fear. The terror of waiting was worse than anything, so she turned to face the soldier. No one. She grasped the fence and forced herself to stand. Gasping, she waited, but again no one called to her, no one pressed a gun to her head.

Holding onto the fence she walked along its perimeter, feeling for a breach. The yotears had stopped patching fences, having little concern about escape or disobedience since the people were completely subdued by starvation and fear. She continued her search until she collapsed in a heap and quietly wept into the dirt. Then she heard the sound of soft laughter behind her.

She pushed herself into a seated position and turned around, looking up into the blurry face of a young soldier. She could see a glint of light on his teeth. He was smiling. He clucked his tongue and said, "Mother, what do you think you're doing? Don't you know no one is allowed into The Little Children's Labor Camp?"

She gaped at him and tried to speak. When he saw how her mouth worked but said nothing, he laughed at her and prodded her shoulder with the rifle. "Come now. Tell me why you are out so late sneaking around the children's compound?"

She put her trembling hand before her face, pleading for mercy. "I am sorry. My daughter is very ill. I heard she's dying. I wanted to see her one last time."

She felt his hand on her arm pulling her up. "Many children have already died. They die for a good cause. Over the course of time, the sacrifice of life to the cause is small compared to the glorious achievement of the goal. Did your re-education do nothing for you?"

How could she tell this young devil what it was like to carry a life for nine months, to feel it growing and moving within? How could she tell him what it was like to bring forth a child in a rush of agony, in a bath of blood and tears, to see its face for the first time, its tiny body reaching to feed and be held? How could he know what it was like to feel care and love grow within you like a second heart? To give the child a name? To watch the child grow and answer to that very name? To hear her call Ma? To feel love returned?

"You have a mother. She loves you like no one else does. She would understand what I do. She would tell you to let me see my child. My child called to me in my dreams."

"I can kill you right here," he said.

"I am the caretaker of the commander's children. I have been very ill. Soon I must return to work. I only wanted to see my child."

The soldier stared at her and squinted his eyes. Her legs shook so badly she could barely stand. "What is your child's name?"

"Tevy. Her name is Tevy."

The soldier took her by her arm and led her to the front of the compound where he unlocked the gate. He took her to a large hut that housed sick children. Everyone was sleeping, even the attendants. Perhaps twenty-five emaciated children filled the hut, all in various stages of dying—skeletal creatures with bloated bellies and arms thin as copper tubing, skin welling with lesions, legs crooked and withered. The soldier led her to her daughter's bed and warned, "You have five minutes. If you are later than that coming out, I will shoot the child and then I will shoot you."

She knelt next to Tevy's bed and called her name. "Oh, Tevy, wake up for a little while and see that your mother has come to you as you asked. Please open your eyes. Tevy, Tevy, answer me. Open your eyes."

Tevy's bluish eyelids fluttered as if they were struggling to open. "Please, Tevy. Ma is here. Ma is with you. Please open your eyes."

She waited, but Tevy did not stir. She wept over her daughter, kissing her cheek, stroking her face and hands, murmuring in her ear. When her time ran out, she knelt over her daughter and kissed her on each eyelid, then the cheeks, and last the lips. She said goodbye and walked outside to meet the soldier, who released her once she was outside the children's compound.

All the way back she wept quietly and murmured incoherently. She begged the gods to take her, for she was losing her mind and her spirit. She no longer cared to live.

～

Next morning she was called to the commander's hut. She was bade to enter and take a seat on a little bench across the room from him. He sat in a large wicker chair, his broad back to a large window so that his face was in shadow. She was terrified. Her desire to die last night was no longer present this morning.

"My children miss you, Met Ona. You will return this afternoon."

"Yes, of course."

"I heard you were in The Little Children's Labor Camp last night."

She clasped her hands in front of her face in supplication. "Yes. I beg your forgiveness. I wanted to see my daughter, Tevy. She's dying. I dreamt that she called me. I beg your forgiveness."

"Do you always listen to your dreams?"

"No. Only certain ones."

"Which ones?" he asked, a smile in his voice.

"The ones that feel very strong."

"Well, look where your dreams have landed you. Maybe you should ignore them."

"Yes, of course. I am a foolish woman."

"But you are worried about your child. That is natural for a mother. Thus the re-education process. Because what is natural is not always good. Yes?"

"Yes, Brother Commander."

He paused for a long time. She dared not raise her eyes and waited in terrified silence. Finally he spoke, his voice like silk. "Ona, do you suppose that there is more to life than fighting to live?"

"I do not know, Commander. Certainly these days there is little else."

"Yes, that's true. Life here is very simple. Here it is reduced to its truest form. No dreams here. Here each will sacrifice for the good of the many. In this there is much suffering. But in the long run Kampuchea will profit."

She said nothing.

"Ona, you look as if you have a question. Ask me your question and don't cheat."

"Even though so many people are dying?"

"Because many people are dying. Purification is hard and difficult work. Yet, I am amazed by a particular phenomenon. Would you like to know what it is, Ona?"

"Yes, sir."

The smile in his voice deepened. "I am amazed that although no single life has a meaning without a culture, without the state, still each life wants so much to continue. To continue for itself. I have seen it so many times. I believe you can kill the entire family, one by one, skin them alive if you want. You can make stew out of the children and force the parents to eat it. The last one left standing will still want to live. Rarely will a person give up, shrivel, and die. For the most part, they will cling to life no matter what. It's shameful how badly we cling to life. That is why we must be subjugated to the state. So as not to be entirely selfish. Don't you think?" He paused and ran the back of his thick hand along his face, still hidden in shadow. Though her head was bowed, she could feel him looking at her. His stare made her tremble. Something in his voice sounded familiar. "Do you still want to live, Ona?"

"Yes. And I want my Tevy to live."

"And your husband and your other child?"

"Yes. Yes. My other child, Kunthea."

"Who do you want to live more? Them or yourself?"

"Them."

He laughed. "Yes, I believe you. But do not think that is a noble impulse, dear comrade. You continue best through your family. Your choice does not violate the rule of clinging. Listen to me carefully, now. If you want to live and you want your family to live, then you must stay away from The Little Children's Labor Camp."

Again she made pleading gestures and begged forgiveness, but he raised his hand to restrain her. "I am not angry. I admire your courage, Ona."

She dared a quick glance into his face, still obscured, still lurking in darkness.

"Do not tremble so. You have nothing to fear from me. My children like you, so I will watch out for you and your family. Here," he commanded. "Take what I have in my hand."

Still seated, he extended his hand out of the shadow and bade her to come toward him. Into her hand he dropped the beautiful shell she had made for her brother.

"It is lovely," he said. "A gift made with great care."

She lowered her head, weeping silently.

"Met Im told me about your brother. Where did he get this?"

"I made it for him when we were young," she answered, choking back tears.

"It must have taken you a long time to make," he said. "Such exquisite attention to detail. I would keep it for myself, but something like this must be given."

She took the shell and clenched it, fighting back tears.

"Some philosophers say everything moves in a circle," he said. "What do you think?"

She offered the shell back to the commander. "It is a

gift for you now," she said. "Please, if there is anything you can do for Tevy. Anything to save her."

He took the gift back and put it in his pocket. "Thank you, Ona. How kind you are. I can see why my little ones are anxious for your return."

～

Under the brazier of the sun, with the buzzards turning in low, slow circles, the inmates toiled with less food to eat every day, the cloth of their shirts growing so thin and frayed that their withered genitals showed. They were too hungry to be ashamed, and there was no fabric to patch the clothing anyway. The prisoners' heads and knees and elbows became absurdly huge on their insect-thin bodies and their eyes bulged in shrinking sockets. Mothers couldn't recognize their kids nor could sons and daughters recognize their parents. Slow death had reduced everyone to the same deformed mud-cake creature. Yet, amazingly, the commander was right; these creatures tenaciously clung to life. Sometimes the guards proved this while amusing themselves with a game called "Find the Center."

The game was simple enough. Herd a group of people together and call for a "volunteer" for a detail that would mean working in unbearable heat near ditches filled with dung-coated, razor-sharp bamboo sticks. There you would see the stinking corpses of your neighbors and friends steaming in the feverish heat, rotting where they had been shot. And you would know that your friends and neighbors had been sent out on a pointless detail just like you. A soldier would stand behind you while you labored and you would wait in terror to die, either by gun or knife or beating. Or in a moment of boredom or anger, the guard might "accidentally" bump you into the ditch where you would be impaled on the stakes. Or perhaps you would return safely from the detail. But then you'd be sent out the next day and the whole cycle of terror would begin again as you were tortured with the suspense of waiting for annihilation.

Naturally, when the yotears played this game, all the people struggled to get to the middle of the circle where they were least likely to be plucked from the crowd. Some of the yotears would laugh in delight at the sight of the mud-cake creatures milling frantically about, pushing against each other as they literally tried to melt into complete anonymity. Sometimes they turned the game inside out and picked a person at the center.

People died in droves and soon death became so commonplace and life so unbearable that Ona sometimes longed to see the black bridge of her dreams, thinking that the next time it appeared she might run and run until she reached the other side.

And yet in her waking life, obedience was her salvation, though she was somewhat surprised to see herself still obeying every command. She felt as if she were watching her actions from a great distance. Her will to live was a puzzle, like the puzzle of why Pol Pot was doing this to her and all the others. What was within her that struggled so fiercely to live? And why? Was it because she wanted her family to live? Or was the commander right? What was it that he said?

I believe you can kill the entire family... The last one left standing will still want to live.

Would she still want to live if she were the last one left? She wondered about this at times, with a detached curiosity. At other times she wondered, with terrible dread, if she were nothing more than a terrified insect burrowing into the mud, clinging to life and trembling before death.

When she thought of these matters, her mind turned hopelessly. Might she now be without a spirit, without the smallest flame burning in her heart? In trying to answer this she looked outward, but what did she see? Starvation, betrayal, and suffocating horror. She looked inward, but what did she see? Darkness, immense unfathomable darkness without even the slightest flicker of a candle light.

Any horror one could imagine, people made happen. Sometimes the soldiers encouraged the children to betray their parents, to report them if they complained against the state or shirked their work. The younger children were especially susceptible to this manipulation and searched among their elders for people with the least calluses on their hands. Occasionally a child's testimony led to a death sentence for a parent, relative, or neighbor, and often the soldiers would let the child perform the execution, first making the condemned one strip and kneel before the soldiers, then placing a pistol in the child's hand and placing the barrel against the head of the elder.

Like the others, Ona pulled down the brim of her palm hat so the soldiers and their spies could not see her react. She prayed to the ancestors and the gods of the fields and the forest to shield her from Pol Pot's soldiers. "Block my enemy from seeing me. Let their minds not have one thought about me or any member of my family."

One morning she was called into the commander's hut. He sat in his wicker chair and smiled at her. Her vision was too hazy to make out his features distinctly.

"I have good news for you. I had Tevy given special medicine. She is doing well. Already she is back to work." He rose from the chair and went to a window, gesturing for her to follow. "Look over there, just at the edge of that field."

Ona stood back a respectful distance from the window.

"I cannot see clearly," she said. "My eyes are very blurry."

"Okay. Let me tell you what I see. She is just beyond the fence happily working for the good of the new state. Later today, you can go by the fence and visit with both of your daughters briefly."

"Thank you for saving my child. I am in your debt."

"Yes, that is true. And I want you to remember that when you are among the others. If you hear any grumbling or learn of any attempts to escape to Thailand, I want you to tell the soldiers. All class enemies must be reported. The reconstruction of our country and culture must come before all personal ties."

She looked down at the floor.

"Ona," he asked with false gentleness, "have you heard what I asked?"

"Yes, I have."

"And what have I asked?"

"You have asked me to report any class enemies."

"And will you?"

"I will," she answered. No other answer existed. She knew, also, that he would be expecting something from her in a short time. And even if she did betray her neighbors, he might kill her and her family anyway. The thought that he had saved Tevy only to condemn her again boggled her mind. She felt as if she were going to pass out. It was not enough to annihilate her. He wanted to first annihilate any hope of spirit, of inward and upward lifting.

"Ona, do you think I am a bad man?"

More torture for her. If she said no, he might kill her for lying. If she said yes, he might kill her for telling the truth. She only wanted to save herself and her family. "What am I to answer to such a question?" she finally responded. "I am blind and sick. I only know you have control over the lives of everyone here."

"I am not a bad man, Ona. I reflect the will of the state. I am nothing more than the servant of the revolution. I pay no attention to dreams or visions. Such is not my duty."

"I understand."

"Now I am among the few who will guide our Democratic Kampuchea to a new era of mastery and independence."

"May you guide us wisely."

"Tomorrow I must set off for Phnom Penh. There is some important work I have to do, but I'll soon return. You will watch over my children while I am away. You will cover the mornings and Met Peuw will cover the rest. Any illegal activities you will report to the soldiers. I expect that you will report soon. Unless you have something to tell us already?"

The sensation of icy cold needles crept up her neck and into her face. Every moment in this man's presence was like being in a wind of flying razors. Every remark he made held the possibility of immediate death for her and her family. She had heard rumors that a new technique of execution was being used throughout the camps. A line of people, single file, was lead up to a soldier armed with a pick axe, each person waiting his turn to lower his head before his executioner, who dispatches him with the dispassion of a civil servant stamping visa applications, splitting heads open like thin-shelled nuts. Another soldier drags the corpse into a large mass grave dug by the condemned. It was like a line at a government bureau, before Cambodia had gone mad. Yes, the whole country exists in a state of murderous insanity. She remembered a child in Khet Kandad whose name she could not recall, a child who rocked back and forth all day long, who pulled out her own hair and bled from self-inflicted wounds. This was Cambodia, a mad child chewing its own flesh.

"I have seen nothing yet. But now I will listen with new ears."

"Yes, yes. That is a good idea."

"Have a prosperous trip," Ona said.

"I'm sure I will," he answered. How did she know he was going to Phnom Penh to help with the killing of more people? Simple really. He was an excellent murderer who enjoyed his work and there was little else to do in Cambodia right now.

That night she told Eng of their new predicament. They both felt that no matter what Ona did, they were all doomed now. The commander had taken note of Ona as he might notice a fly buzzing in his room. He might play with her for a little while, but sooner or later he would smash her and her loved ones.

"We must escape before he returns," Eng said.

"We cannot escape. We are too weak. And Tevy is not well, though they are feeding her more now. And Kunthea has lost all her good cheer."

Thinking about how the children had reached for her with outstretched hands calling, "Ma, Ma, don't go so soon," made her weep, but Eng could offer no words of comfort. There were no words of comfort left. Any word of hope seemed like a lie, a delusion that might flit through the mind as one stood before a cocked pistol: perhaps the gun will jam and I will be freed.

"What will we do about my being asked to spy?" She looked into his eyes and saw the question echoed there. She began to shake, at first with slight tremors, but then uncontrollably. He reached for her with his withered arms and held her close. "What do you say about this, husband?"

"I can only say I love you and always will. We will be together in another life."

"It is this life I am talking about, Eng. How can I spy? I cannot spy. What shall we do?"

"I have an idea!" he said, clapping his trembling hands together. "I will try to steal nuts and fruits from the edge of the forest. With the commander gone, you might encourage his kids to give you more food. It might be enough for us to gather our strength to run. We'll sneak what we can to the kids."

She looked at him questioningly and he nodded. "We might be caught and killed, Ona. But what other choice do we have?"

"But what will we do if I'm asked to report someone? It can happen at any time. It can happen tomorrow. What will I say?"

The anguish in her voice silenced Eng. He looked at yet another layer of grief etching itself into her face. What would she say to the iron face of authority when it demanded she betray a neighbor? What could he possibly say?

He looked down at the dirt between them and said nothing.

∾

Occasionally she saw her daughters at work in the

fields and felt relieved that they were still alive. Then she'd think of her son safe in Thailand with her parents. Surely he was safe for she could think of no other possibility. How glad she was that he didn't see what was happening to his sisters. The yotears again had stopped allowing the children to come to the fence before dark. In the fields she could never get close enough to talk to them and she dared not wave. Sometimes her daughters and other children in The Little Children's Labor Camp would be sent to work in another province, and she would hear nothing of them for days until they returned. When her daughters were gone, so was her spirit, flying along with them, turning her inner emptiness into a vacuum, her heart into a bitter, black stone. And she would ask herself, Why do I still worry after them? They are dead. I am dead. Eng is dead. We are already dead. But still she worried for her babies.

If her children died, she and Eng should commit suicide. Easy enough, just spit in a soldier's face. But in her clearer moments she realized that the time for suicide for her, for all the people in the camp, had passed long ago. Suicide or even passive resistance required a strength of resolve that had been depleted by the physical and mental torture endured for so many months. She had entered a realm of hopelessness well beyond the hopelessness of the suicidal mind.

One afternoon she and Eng were sent to work in the fields together. It was raining, and despite the occasional fruit Eng stole for his wife and himself, both of them were so weak and frail from hunger neither could dig nor carry heavy loads. And so they were sent to move small rocks from one place to another. Eng happened to look up and motioned to Ona. "Look."

She followed the direction of his finger to the top of a tall tree where large brown nuts grew. "I want to get some," he said.

"It's too tall. You will not be able to climb. And if a soldier sees you, he will kill us both."

"We've discussed this already." He uttered a choked laugh. "Isn't it something? The demon yotears distribute one tin of rice for twelve people. Yet the fruit rots on the trees and we're not allowed to pick it."

"Eng, please. Let's return."

"I'm getting us those nuts."

She looked into his eyes for the first time in several weeks. His face was dried and cracked from the sun and his arms were thin as reeds. But for a moment she saw in him the Eng she knew from her youth, the brazen young man whose eyes invited her to dance on the large porch in his mother's house and laugh with him beneath the smiling moon. She saw in his desiccated face a spark of determination to still live with dignity, and so she nodded. "Yes, the nuts might be good."

She was surprised that he was able to climb the tree and happy to see him gather large handfuls of nuts and wrap them in a filthy rag that he tied around his wrist. But on the way down he lost his balance and fell, landing a few feet in front of her. She cried out and ran to him. His eyes were half opened and he was gasping for breath. A little blood trickled from his mouth, but he placed the nuts in Ona's hands. She held him in her arms, rocking him. "This is the end," she said. "There is no more."

But he looked up and smiled at her. "I'm okay. I just have to catch my breath a little. I bit my tongue when I hit the ground."

Her eyes widened. He had fallen far and he was already so weak. How could he not have been hurt?

"Ona, I blacked out for a moment when I hit the ground. Our son appeared. His skin was blackened and the whites of his eyes were yellow. He is very sick. But he told me we will all be together again."

She brought her hand up to her mouth, "No. He can't be sick. He's in Thailand."

"Perhaps."

"He must be." She began to weep.

Eng gently touched her shoulder. "He said we'll be

together again."

"Does that mean life for us?"

Eng sat up and smiled. Despite his fall, he looked better than he had in months. "I believe we will be together again."

"Why has this happened, Eng?"

Eng shook his head. "I don't know why. Perhaps there is no reason."

Ona wiped tears away. "How can this happen? How can children kill their own parents? How can the soldiers be so evil? How can there not be a reason?"

"That is the hardest part," he agreed. "To feel so betrayed and to have no answer why. Why have we been sent into the fields? Why do the soldiers kill us? I don't know why."

They looked into each other's eyes. Silence provided the only answer to such a question. At least the silence did not lie.

∾

The days passed like worms crawling up a tree. People died either from illness or execution. When Ona wasn't on a shift with the commander's children, she worked with a group of old women spinning cotton. Her sight faded worse than ever, a continual blur now, shades of gray and brown with occasional pinpoints of light dazzling her vision and giving her terrible headaches, the feeling of needles behind her eyes. Luckily, she did not need her eyes to spin. Yet, when her vision was at its worst, her mind had moments of great clarity in which she was able to think something through, deferring her fear, until the process was complete. And she owed this new development to the commander.

Despite her abhorrence at the thought of spying, she found her mind storing memories of the things people said that could be construed as subversive to the new state. It was as if a part of her had already decided that she would spy, that she would do anything to protect her own interests. The commander had described it quite perfectly: rarely will a person give up, shrivel and die. For the most part they will cling to life no matter what. It's shameful how badly we cling to life. Yes, shameful. Yet, alongside this desire to live at all costs was the desire to be the person one was meant to be. And that person for Ona was one who would never spy on innocent people. Report enemies of state! Then everyone should be reported, for all the prisoners of the camp were enemies of the state. She could not possibly imagine a survivor having anything good to say about the state. Furthermore, if a state was a collection of people who worked for a common good, then the soldiers were enemies of the state, too.

What a thing to say when asked to report: we are all enemies of the state, Commander, and we should all be executed! We have so wronged our country that it should be emptied of every single one of us. Let the earth be nourished on the bad blood of our self-hatred.

Still she remembered snatches of conversation, grumbling, complaining, and outright expressions of contempt. And so, whenever that thing inside her had its way and remembered what it needed to survive, she countered it by also recalling something that could be construed as a self-betrayal. If she were to say something that would betray an innocent, then she would also say something to betray herself. *After all, I, too, hate the state.* In this way, she fought off the tendency to become a thing and kept the books balanced.

Clarity begot clarity. Each time she acknowledged her desire to spy, she told herself that she would not spy. You will not spy. You will not betray an innocent person. If you do, you'll have nothing left. Your spirit will leave your heart forever. Then you'll be made to betray your husband, your kids. In the end, death will not be enough for you. You will not spy. You will not betray an innocent.

The eldest crone in the circle of spinning women mentioned that some young men and women of pale complexions had been caught and killed at the edge of the forest. Whose children were they, the elder mused, and why had they been carrying foreign suitcases? Everyone in Ona's family had a pale complexion. She thought immediately of her cousins, uncles, aunts. Perhaps someone had come looking for her. Perhaps her son was with them. Perhaps her son had been killed. The women told Ona where the bodies were, but Ona was too frightened to go look. Besides, she might hardly be able to see them. And if one of the bodies were her son, how could she possibly go on?

The soldiers called a meeting that evening, telling everyone that rations would have to be cut further because people were not working hard enough. The regime had made great sacrifices to improve the lives of all and sacrifices were necessary to build a new country under Pol Pot. Someday everyone would be prosperous, but now hard work was necessary and punishment would be swift for anyone slacking in their great responsibility to the new order. Independence from all countries and mastery over its destiny was the state's complete focus. Rice production must increase. All production must increase. The harvest had to be brought in quickly. Quickly! There was little time to waste. Everyone had to work to their limit to make this happen. No exceptions. Rumor had it that the commander would return to the camp soon and the harvest had to be in before his return.

After the meeting Ona found herself walking toward a soldier, unable to restrain herself. It was as if she were in a dream of how she would die. All eyes were on her as she approached the soldier, looking directly into his eyes. Surely she would be killed, but in that moment it no longer mattered.

"What has happened to my son?" she asked in a clear voice. The meeting fell silent and she waited for a bullet or a bayonet. Or perhaps she would be tortured first, though certainly not raped. All of the women, even the youngest, looked quite horrible now, like wasted corpses come to life for a short time before returning to their graves. One soldier had casually commented that the women were disappearing into the spaces of their own wombs.

The soldier stared at her, his wild, narrow eyes opening wide.

"My son," she repeated. "I want to know what has become of him."

"Mother, why do you wish for your son? I am your son. Your former son is in another village. He has other mothers, but I am here with you now." He fixed her with a taunting smile. "How can you ask for your son, when I, your son here and now, stand before you?"

One of the women pulled her aside after the meeting. "That was not wise," she warned. "You think because you mind the commander's children that you will be saved. This puts you at greater risk! The soldiers will tell him what you said when he returns. You will be killed. Your family will be killed too."

"I don't care anymore."

"Liar! You care. You would still betray anyone to save yourself and your family."

Ona nodded. "Yes, that's probably true. Take care not to say anything bad about Pol Pot or his sons. I have been told to keep watch."

The woman's eyes widened. "And will you?"

"If I tell you I will not, you certainly won't believe me. So why ask?"

When the woman looked away in fear, Ona touched her lightly on the shoulder. "No, no, Mother. I will not betray you or anyone else. Better to save the flame still burning within than to relinquish it for more of this miserable existence. I hate Pol Pot. I hate his sons. I hate the new order."

The women gaped at her.

Ona managed a smile. "You know," she continued, "I was thinking about something. Do you recall how we would greet each other when Prince Sihanouk reigned? Do you remember? We would say, 'How many children have you?' Then with Lon Nol, 'Are you in good health?' When

Khmer Rouge came, we asked at first, 'How much food do you get under the cooperative?' And when these devils pass back into the earth, do you know what we'll say in salutation? We'll say, 'How many of your family are still alive?'"

The woman shook her head and shrugged. "My tears are dried up. I wonder to myself how much more I can take. And still I find I can take more and more. It seems there is no end to what I can take."

~

That night Ona dreamed at last of the black bridge, and now she ran along its impossible length with all her might, determined to cross over and never return. "I've had enough! I've had enough!" she shouted to the sky as she ran. "Please, please, take me! Finish me now!"

The bridge arched higher and higher as she ran toward its apex. She stopped and touched the hot black girders and looked to the sky where the sun burned like an evil eye. She could feel the steel, the heat, the steamy air pressing her body on every side. She realized that though her body was sleeping on her mat, this place where she stood was as real as the camp, the forest, the soldiers, the hunger that consumed her even as she slept. The bridge was so high it could run over mountain peaks. Looking down at the ocean miles below she could see it curving in the shape of the world.

A mist cloaked the road before her, and as she walked slowly through it, she felt the damp gather around her legs. When she emerged, she came to a gaping break in the bridge right at its highest point. The bridge continued on the other side of the gap, too far to step or jump. She peered over the edge and saw the ocean below as one might see it from the clouds. When she looked up to the other side where the bridge continued, she saw her brother sitting on the edge of the road where the bridge ended, his legs dangling free. She sat down on the edge and let her legs dangle too. He waved to her and smiled. "Sister, it's so good to see you."

"What happened here?"

"I don't know, dear heart. It was never finished, I suppose."

"How can I reach you?"

"If you were a swan, you could fly across."

"I have no wings, Ket."

Her brother looked beautiful in a magnificent yellow robe adorned with ornate geometrical designs in brilliant colors, his wrists, ankles, and neck decked with many large jewels. His eyes were bright and fierce, like a tiger's or a hawk's.

"You can go no further, sister. You must go back."

"I don't want to go back. Why can't I cross?"

"Crossing time is not yours to decide."

"Ket. Ket!" she called out, throwing her arms up. "Why! Why does the mother eat her own children? Why does she do it?"

He smiled and shook his head from side to side. "The ocean is beautiful, Ona. The sky, too, is beautiful. And the rich earth awaits us, dear sister. Mother's children eat each other."

"I could never do what the soldiers do."

"No, you are consecrated, sister. Your heart is pure as gold. Yet, the soldiers are not separate from you or the others. None are blameless and all flee from death. The endless web spreads on all sides. The soldiers fit their prisoners like an axle fits its wheel."

"I miss you, Ket. I miss you so much."

When she finally opened her eyes, she found herself on her mat, awake in her room bright with moonlight. "Please Ket, let me go back. I want to go back."

As Ona sat on her mat, images burst into her mind and she closed her eyes to better see them. A neighbor had said that the yotears were digging a large pit at the edge of the forest. At once she understood that pit was to be the home of their corpses. The soldiers planned to kill everyone in the camp as soon as the harvest was in! As her eyes closed tighter, she concentrated more deeply. A fresh image burst into her mind like lightning. She saw other soldiers, the Vietnamese, close by, pushing through the forests of her country, invading the land, searching for the yotears. Could it be true? Was her country on the verge of being freed from the iron grip of Pol Pot?

$\sim$

How could she find the Vietnamese soldiers, if indeed they were even in the country? She could hardly see in the glare of daylight, let alone the gloom of night. Yet she felt calm and fearless for the first time since before she had seen the black Buddha weep four years ago. She was no longer worried about the spiked pits, the yotears, or the forests. She left the shack quickly without waking her husband and made her way toward the forest, groping with her hands stretched out in front of her. If she didn't quickly find the help she envisioned, the soldiers in the camp might kill her husband and even her daughters. In the blurry black distance she saw a shadowy form. It looked like a small tree. It appeared to move. She followed it.

All night long she moved through the dense foliage, tangling in vines and cutting her face on branches. Every few yards she marked a tree with a sharp stone so the soldiers would have a trail back to the enemy. Later the moon moved behind some clouds but the shape she'd been following still shone faintly in the blurry gloom. She pushed on, still marking trees, confident, at first, that she would find the soldiers.

But as the hours passed she became weary and breathless. By morning she was so exhausted that she collapsed and could go no further. The little tree that had seemed to guide her had abandoned her in the light of dawn. She rolled over on her back and looked up between the trees as the sky lightened. She closed her eyes and prayed to see Ket again. She struggled to her feet a few times, walked a step or two, and fell down. Relieved to be close to death, she shut her eyes. Her husband, children, her family, what did it all matter now? All her suffering dissolved and she felt within herself a floating peace that surrounded her heart like the night mist. She lay in the forest all day and slept.

She was awakened by voices hovering over her. At first she thought they were the voices of guardian spirits come to take her across the black bridge at last. But it was the Vietnamese soldiers who found her dying on the forest floor. When she whispered that she had escaped from a work camp to look for them, they gave her water and a little rice. Carrying her on a makeshift stretcher and using the marks she'd cut into the trees to guide them back to the camp, they cut through the forest and spoke excitedly about the coming battle.

Feeling a little revived, she pleaded with them to hurry.

"The yotears will kill everyone. Soon it will be too late."

"Don't worry, hag," they answered. "We are the true liberators of the people of Kampuchea. Vietnam is Kampuchea's older brother."

She lay back on the stretcher and listened to their boasting. All young boys, the tribes of Lon Nol, Pol Pot, and now the Vietnamese. Liberators. Murderers. Fools. Young men blind to life, manipulated by older men pledged to the destruction of life. Perfect instruments of ignorance.

They carried Ona through the forest all day and in the afternoon they were joined by another large group of Vietnamese soldiers. Now the group outnumbered the enemy, two to one.

Toward evening the soldiers arrived at the edge of Ona's camp and huddled in small groups while their commander moved from group to group whispering instructions for the attack. An attachment broke away and circled the camp from the other side of the forest edge. Ona sat up. Through the brush she could dimly see the camp. She looked around for her husband and beyond to the fence of The Little Children's Labor Camp. She prayed that none of the inmates would be injured in the attack. It was nearly evening and most of the people were in their pathetic shelters. Some yotears were standing outside the huts;

others were leaning against the worn and dusty fenders of trucks, talking and smoking. When both Vietnamese flanks moved in from either side of the compound the yotears were caught completely off guard.

In the initial rush of the attacking force, a storm of automatic-weapon fire brought down many of the yotears, bright bloody stars bursting from their chests and limbs. The yotears ran for cover in the huts and compounds while the few inmates standing outside dropped to the ground and covered their heads. The well-trained Vietnamese soldiers rushed into the camp with a great war cry and fired their weapons with deadly accuracy. Like so many of the people they had tortured and killed, the yotears were screaming for mercy and receiving none. Some fell wounded, crying and moaning in the dirt, raising their hands to beg their executioners, but the bullets ripped them to pieces. As Ona watched them die, one after another, she did not feel the angry sense of happiness that is revenge. Instead, a numbing sorrow flooded her heart and she lay back on her cot and wept.

Some of the yotears had run into the huts, but the Vietnamese ruthlessly pursued them, gunning them down where they hid. Some of the inmates joined the attacking soldiers, pointing and shouting to fleeing yotears. Even the few who ran into the forest were tracked down and shot.

The battle hardly lasted ten minutes and five yotears remained alive, throwing down their weapons and surrendering to the Vietnamese. They knelt down before their captors, holding their clasped hands in front of them, begging for their lives.

The battle over, many of the inmates of the camp came out of hiding, jeering at the captured yotears, calling for their immediate death. Ona stood shakily on her feet, seeing this familiar scene, sick with it, this eternal image of man broken by man. The commander of the Vietnamese force stood over the five men, sneering at their pleas. He took a revolver from his holster and walked behind each man, casually shooting each in the head while the people cheered. The Vietnamese also cheered, waving brightly colored rags to declare their victory.

The liberated prisoners staggered around the field, marveling at the scene around them. Some of the people spat on the well-fed corpses of Pol Pot's sons, while others stepped over them like bags of garbage as they slowly walked toward The Little Children's Labor Camp to collect their kids.

Ona looked around. Since the night of her journey her vision had improved. Whispering to herself she said, "In a moment everything has changed once again. In a single moment!" She walked over to the bodies of two yotears. One had reveled in cruelty. The other had done his duty reluctantly and was even known for small acts of kindness. Both lay next to each other like brothers, their arms touching, their heads cocked at severe angles. Their difference in life no longer mattered in death. Looking at them now, it was as though neither had ever existed.

She felt her husband's hand grasp her arm. "Ona. What are you looking at? Haven't you seen enough death? Let us find Kunthea and Tevy."

Ona and Eng stumbled through the children's compound calling out for their daughters. Both were huddled in the corner of a hut, trying to hide under some dirty rags. When they saw their parents, they ran toward them. Weeping with anguish and relief, the parents embraced the two little skeletons who cried out, "Ma! Dad!" and nuzzled against their bodies. They might never grow as they once could have, but at least they were alive.

They stayed on a few more days, until Ona gathered enough strength to return to Svay Sisophon. Before leaving the camp, she and Eng were called into the commander's hut and questioned by one of the Vietnamese leaders.

"Did you know that the entire camp was to be executed?"

She hesitated before answering. But what lie could she possibly tell? "I had an idea," she answered.

He laughed. "Ideas are not allowed under Pol Pot. No ideas. No praying. No Buddha. No weeping for the dead. No emotions. Your re-education obviously failed."

"It's not my fault," she answered.

"Well, you probably saved your neighbors. We found documents that said the entire village was to be destroyed following the harvest. They were going to do it in a very efficient manner. They dug a large pit in a clearing in the forest. Then each person would kneel at the edge of the pit and get a pick axe in the skull. That way they would fall directly into the hole. Keep a few alive to cover it all up. Then kill them as well. Very tidy." He paused to light a cigarette. "You have us to thank for your lives."

Both she and her husband bowed repeatedly until the soldier raised his hand and asked, "Do you know where the leader of this place is? Met Commander. Where is he?"

Ona said, "No, but before he left he said he had important work to do in Phnom Penh."

The soldier sneered. "Yes, important work for Pol Pot, that Chinese puppet. He was probably sent to Tuol Sleng. That is a high school used as an interrogation facility. Many go in, but none come out."

"Well, I don't know where he is now," she said.

"Hopefully he is dead, as will be the rest of Pol Pot's dogs!"

Rocco Lo Bosco

Liberation

Following a long painful journey on foot, in which they scavenged wild berries from the forest to stay alive, Ona and her family returned to Svay Sisophon. The house they had lived in was wrecked but still a palace compared to the hut in the work camp. Hoping to find her son, Ona left for the market almost as soon as she was home. Skeletal people were milling around, looking for loved ones, their shuffling feet raising clouds of yellow dust. The weathered stalls had fallen to pieces, and the road was deeply rutted with tire tracks. Ona dimly saw a withered young man walking shakily toward her. He told her he was looking for his family and asked her if she knew an Ona Ny. She threw her arms around him and began to weep. If she hadn't heard his voice, she would have never recognized her son.

"I am your mama," she said. Both had been so altered

by starvation that neither recognized the other except by the sound of the voice.

After their initial embrace, they pulled away and looked into each other's eyes. His jaw dropped as he intently examined her shrunken face. The dreaded moment had come.

"Father?" he asked. "Sisters?"

"Alive," she said. "They are home."

He sighed with relief.

"Mama and Papa?" she asked.

"Grandma and Grandpa are dead, Ma. We got close to the border. Grandpa stepped on a land mine. Within minutes we were swarmed by yotears. They shot Grandma, who was still wailing. They spared me. Put me into another work camp near the border of Thailand. They destroyed all radio communication. We starved. They worked us to death. I'm sorry, Ma. We almost made it to Thailand."

She nodded, eyes closed, holding onto her son.

"How about Uncle Ket and his family?" Ding asked.

Tears ran from her closed eyes, but she said nothing.

"Dead?" he asked.

She nodded.

"Everyone?' he asked, a tremor in his voice.

She nodded again. "Dead," she whispered. "All dead."

They held each other gently, swaying with grief and vertigo. Few tears were shed for few tears were left. Both numb from anguish, news of more death hardly surprised either of them. In fact finding out someone was still alive was more shocking than discovering they had died. Everywhere similar scenes were being enacted. Thousands of people wandered ghost-like through the bone fields of Cambodia, numbly searching out family members and inquiring about lost loved ones. Not one family in Cambodia escaped the brutal years under the red Khmer.

When the entire family was reunited in their old home, Ona steamed some Red Cross rice and put out cut fruit on a large plate. Though Ding had been separated from the family for four years, conversation was sparse. Ona did most of the talking, inquiring after friends and neighbors, talking about the new government and warning everyone to eat more slowly so they would not become ill. As she ate she looked into the face of each family member. Everyone had deep frown lines and wrinkles running through their foreheads and surrounding their dull and shocked eyes; their mouths turned down as if a permanent frown had been carved into their faces. When someone did occasionally smile their face looked like a smiling mask of pain. Here in the flesh of her family she surveyed a record of insane devastation. Even the youngest, Kunthea, looked like a little old lady, her face gaunt, prominent lines of the skull showing in the forehead, chin, and cheeks. Little Kunthea, she was already a hundred years old.

For a moment she saw the four of them as an image of bones, skulls, vertebrae, and ribs, already dead like all the others. And then, recalling her dream of the black bridge, she looked again and saw them as creatures of radiant light emanating from the sun. Would any of them have the strength to stand beyond the hellish fields of Kampuchea? I wish I could give you all my heart, she thought looking at them sadly. How I wish I could take your pain away. I wish I could make you forget all that has happened in the fields of death.

But she could not. "We are together," she said. "It will be okay now."

Ding-Toy looked up from his plate with a bitter frown. "We are not together, Mother. We have been cut into pieces."

She smiled at her son and nodded. "Then, let us care for what remains."

∽

In the following days, Ona decided they must escape the country. But soon after Ona announced her decision, Ding was appointed superintendent of the town. He also became enamored of a young nurse who had seen her entire family executed in a labor camp. "Why the rush to leave?" he asked.

"The new government is the same truck of death. They're just switching drivers, Ding-Toy. If we stay here, we will all be killed."

"Mother, the Vietnamese are in charge of our country now. It will be different. Pol Pot is ruined. That is just your fear talking."

Grabbing his hands in hers, she looked at him fiercely. "Yes. It is my fear talking. When the statue of Buddha wept, my fear spoke and I didn't listen. Now I do. Do not be a complacent fool. The Democratic Kumpuchea under Pol Pot, the People's Republic of Kampuchea under Vietnam—do you really suppose in the long run it will make a difference? The ruthlessness and stupidity will continue, my son. We can expect nothing from the government. Already they have us working too much again. To rely on others is to be uneasy. Haven't you learned that yet? We cannot stay here."

Ding-Toy looked at his mother with puzzled interest. "Mother, you've changed."

"Yes."

"How?"

She smiled at him and considered her answer. "I am awake."

Ding chuckled and shook his mother's hands. "Are you a Buddha now?"

"Ding-Toy, I am your mother. And your mother is telling you that the family cannot stay in Svay Sisophon. Will you not listen to her?"

"Let me think about it, Mother."

"Please think quickly," she answered. "There's not much time."

Eng suggested that Ding marry his girlfriend, the nurse. The Vietnamese would give the family a day off from work to celebrate, and they could use the holiday to escape to Thailand. Under pressure from both parents, especially Ona, Ding finally gave in and agreed to lead the family to Thailand. Ona and Eng packed what valuables they could carry, including some gold that had been stored behind a wall in the porch. Ding married the girl, and shortly before the dawn of their nuptial holiday, Ona and her family entered the forest, falling in with a group of twenty villagers also heading for the border. The group walked single file, each person stepping slowly and carefully in the footstep of the person in front of them to avoid land mines and booby traps. Ona insisted she walk in the front of the line.

Eng and Ding argued with her. "Are you crazy?" Ding asked. "You're still half blind and weak as a crippled frog. Father, speak to her."

Eng looked at his wife with sad eyes. "Please, Ona."

Ding was angry with both parents; his mother's behavior was bizarre and his father seemed utterly docile and bewildered. Both his sisters were like turtles hidden deep within their shells, their bruised, watery eyes peering out fearfully. Seeing them cringe at a sudden movement or an unexpected sound made him boil with rage. They had probably been raped before they had become too thin to appeal to the yotears. He had not suffered as much as the rest of the family and had never reached the final stage of starvation. He had many fantasies about slaughtering yotears, and his nights were haunted by terrifying dreams of people being stripped of their skin by huge machines with wheels of barbed wire and gears with razors poking from the sides.

"I want to go in front," Ona said. "I am the slowest. It makes sense for the slowest to go in front; that way no one will have to wait for me to catch up. More time is lost that way."

"I do not want to lose you after all this time," Eng begged. "Besides, you can hardly see."

"My eyesight is improving. If you wish, you can walk behind me."

No one knew how long the journey would take, or if they had enough dried fish to bribe the Vietnamese soldiers they met along the way, or if they had enough rice, or enough gold. Once they walked past what they believed to be the last area of booby traps, the group broke into smaller groups, each traveling at its own speed. Ona's pace slowed to a crawl. During the second night of travel, she ran a fever and implored the family to leave her behind.

"It's okay," she told Eng, who wept with his daughters, and Ding-Toy, who was red-faced with fury at his mother's weakness.

"Ding, won't you release me now? I can go no further."

Ding hoisted Ona onto his shoulders. "No, Mother, I will not let death take you. The goddamn yotears have already taken enough."

Just before the border, they stopped to rest in a small clearing in the forest with another group of travelers. Ona had a blister on her foot the size of a small egg. She went to sit down against a tree to rest when her body froze, knees bent, legs spread. She was unable to stand or sit. It looked as though she was locked into the position of relieving herself. Even the grim expression on her face suggested a difficult bowel movement.

Ding-Toy laughed at her. "Look at my little Buddha mama taking a dump in the forest. Is this the face of an enlightened one who wished to go to a foreign country?"

Despite her pain, Ona laughed, and with that she felt something relaxing in her back. Thinking about what Ding-Toy had said while feeling her back pain diminish made her laugh even more. It felt so good to laugh. How long had it been? She laughed and laughed and soon she was able to move quite freely again. The fever subsided and the next morning the family set out for a huge camp hosting thousands of refugees across the border. When they finally arrived, they were given a small strip of land and a piece of plastic and told by the Thai soldiers, "Build your home."

Eng and Ding gathered some bamboo to hold the plastic, but a storm stole the plastic and their first night in the camp was spent with the rainy sky as their cover. Still, they were out of harm's way and had food to eat, given to them by the camp attendants. For the first time in years, they slept without death sitting on their chests. The next day a Cambodian family furnished them with some small tents for shelter. Ding and his father began building a small shelter out of bamboo and tree branches.

Ding sent a letter to distant cousins in California, who had moved to America right before the Khmer Rouge had taken over the country, petitioning them to sponsor the family. The Nys went on a waiting list. Though their new camp did have food, the conditions were difficult and dangerous. Thai soldiers would roam the camp at night and occasionally rape a woman. Peddlers allowed in the camp by the soldiers were often thieves and frequently beat their victims. The people still lived as prisoners, though not like before. There was food and medicine and a chance to live.

An American man helping refugees took Ona to a hospital, a one room hut in a clearing, where a doctor put drops in Ona's eyes and made her read an eye chart. Other women sitting on the bench next to her averted their eyes when someone spoke to them. A French doctor asked Ona why the women would not even incline their gaze toward a person speaking to them.

"They are so terrified," Ona said. "They look straight ahead because they are hoping no more bad things will happen."

He nodded grimly, his thick glasses catching the light. "And you, how is it that you do not look straight ahead?"

"I have been fortunate," she answered. "Are many of them blind?"

"Yes, and we don't know why," the doctor answered. "There appears to be nothing wrong with their eyes. And though you seem to have more vision than they, your eyes should see perfectly. I can see nothing wrong."

"That's because you look for harm to our eyes."

He bent down to scrutinize her closely. "I don't understand."

She looked into his face and smiled gently. "Our hearts are crushed by what we have clearly seen, and so we can no longer bear to see clearly."

~

Month after month, Ona's family waited. Everyone grew edgy with waiting, except Ona. Each day Ding-Toy would walk to a large bulletin board on the far side of the camp to see if the family's name had been listed among those sponsored to go to America, and each day he would return home frustrated, angrily wondering how much longer this half-life would continue.

One day he shouted at his mother, "See! I was made the superintendent of our village. They were going to send me away to school. I could have made something of myself. But instead we live in this shit! We are names on a list of names that does not end. Dad sits around in a half-dead state. The girls live like frightened rabbits. I peddle fish. My wife is pregnant and what future can I hope to give her in this stinking camp! And you...you are a half-blind fool! We should have never left."

Ona turned a gentle smiling gaze on her son. "You call your mother a fool. How disrespectful. You shame yourself with such behavior. How many more have died in

Cambodia since we left? What do the new refugees say? Thousands more. Tens of thousands, they say. Too many have died and we would have been among them. You grow tired of waiting. But are we not always waiting for something? All our lives we wait, everyone waits. If you're tired of waiting, live your life without the waiting."

"Look at the nonsense you talk," Ding-Toy retorted. "How do you know we would have been killed? You do not know. And how can I stop waiting if all of life is waiting?"

"Look at your mother if you do not know," she replied gently. "I wait and yet I do not wait. I have no need to raise my voice and call you names. You are my son and I have loved you always. Yet, see how you speak to me? You have forgotten who you are and who I am. You have forgotten and that's why you're so impatient and angry. So you blame the waiting for your impatience. But your impatience is with yourself, with your bad memory. With your restless anger. With your sleepy love. And so the waiting seems unbearable."

"Oh, thank you, Buddha, for your sage advice. I must go and meditate on it now," Ding shouted with great frustration. But already a smile had crept onto his face. His insufferable mother was always endearing to him and in truth he loved her ferociously.

Ona smiled and nodded. "You know, if you were a little nicer, you'd remind me of your Uncle Ket."

One day Ona and Eng were in a makeshift market-place outside the camp when Eng excitedly whispered, "Ona, do you see that monk by the cart?"

Ona's still-blurry vision was aided by the noon light, and gradually she brought the man's face into focus. "That's one of the soldiers from the work camp. I recognize him."

"Yes, yes. I've heard he has killed many innocent people. Suk?"

"Yes," she answered calmly. "Suk. It's him. Look at the hypocrite hiding in the robes of the wise. He might have been the very one who led my brother and his family into the woods."

Most of the soldiers who had guarded Pol Pot's concentration camps had gone into hiding, because once exposed, they were frequently beaten to death by angry mobs of peasants for the atrocities they had committed. Those memories lived within the people like a second body made of iron. No future hope or possibility could mitigate the pain of what they had endured, and so most were condemned to be haunted by a past that continually drained them of energy and cheer. Though they survived the camp, their lives had been taken away, and many of them envied the ones who had died.

Before Eng could stop her, Ona walked toward the man, drawing close, narrowing her eyes and staring at him so hard that he stopped.

"Are you the man who killed my brother and his family?"

"What are you saying?" he asked. "I am a monk. I practice non-violence. I have killed no one."

A crowd gathered. Ona raised an accusing finger and smiled at him. "Sweet words now from a liar and a murderer of helpless children. My brother was a good man. You killed him for no reason. You killed his wife. You killed his children."

The man backed away from Ona in terror and the crowd closed behind him so he could not run. He waved his hands wildly and turned round and round as he uttered his protests to the crowd. "This woman is crazy. I've done nothing. I am a monk. I am innocent. I've harmed no one."

Ona walked up to the man, bringing her face within a few inches of his. "You are a world destroyer, full of pride and arrogance," she whispered fiercely. "You are a slaughterer of children. You are the shame of humanity. You bring harm to heaven and earth. I accuse you of killing my brother and his family."

A young man with white hair and an old face came

forward in the crowd and stood by Ona. "I know this man. I did not recognize him in robes. But months ago he and I drank together. He bragged to me about being a soldier for Pol Pot."

The crowd moved in on the man, shouting and stirring like a gathering storm. Ona turned to them to speak. "Do not harm him," she warned in a small but clear voice that carried over the heads of the angry people. "You become the enemy that you slay. Leave his fate to the gods."

Turning back to the man, who had now fallen on his backside, she put her face close to his. "Do you know why you killed so many? Tell me. Why did you do it?"

He stared at her, terror in his eyes. "I am innocent."

"If you say that again, I'll call the crowd down on you. You are not innocent. You are a son of Pol Pot. You have been recognized. Is that not true?"

The man averted his eyes. "Yes. Yes. It's true."

"Why, then? Why did you do it?"

He kept his eyes down but they appeared to look inward. He looked at her again and opened his mouth as if to speak. But he said nothing.

"Run now. Run away," she said finally in a loud voice, "But know that we have seen you. Know that our faces and the faces of those whom we loved and you slew for pleasure will haunt you for the rest of your life. Our hearts hold your evil heart prisoner."

~

A neighbor told Ding-Toy about the yotear disguised as a monk. "Your mother cursed him. The yotear ran like the wind."

"Do you know where is he now?" Ding asked.

"I hear he's hiding out on the other side of the camp in his little hut. It's right on the forest's edge. He'll probably flee into the forest because the people know about him."

Ding faked nonchalance and told the neighbor he had to go home, but as soon as he was out of the man's sight, he circled back and crossed the river. After a few casual inquiries, he located the yotear's hut. He broke off the large end of a fallen tree branch and crept on hands and knees toward the hut.

Ding crawled beneath the opening in the thatch that served as a window. Kneeling up very slowly, he lifted his head to look inside. The man was curled on his side, clothed in the robes of a monk, sleeping on the floor. A bundle of rags was tied up and mounted on a stick in the corner of the hut.

Ding looked to make sure no one was around. Then he boldly strode into the hut and prodded the man with his foot.

The man jumped to a seated position and looked at Ding-Toy. Clasping his hands in front of his face, he said, "Please, sir, I am a monk. Do not harm me."

Ding sneered at him. "You are a yotear hiding in a monk's robes."

"No, no. I am a monk. Please, do not harm me!"

"You are a monk?" Ding asked. "Did you study Buddhist scripture, monk?"

"Yes. Of course. All monks must study Buddhist teachings."

Ding crouched down so he was eye-to-eye with the man. The phony monk had a small rat-like face, eyes the size of pebbles, sharp little teeth. He looked healthy, a bit plump, no recent victim of any work camp. Toy held the wooden stump lightly in his hands and positioned it between his legs. "Good. Tell me then, what are the four noble truths of the Buddha?"

Ding smiled meanly when he saw the man's eyes film with tears.

"All is suffering. That is the first. Right?"

The man nodded. "I don't remember," he said.

"I see. Then tell me the four noble truths of Pol Pot. Do you know them?"

The man clasped his trembling hands in front of his face.

"You don't recall them either, murderer, do you? I'll tell you then," Ding said standing up over the man, who bowed his head. "The first is, Drive the people into the fields. The second is, Starve the people until their bones poke through their flesh. The third is, Work the people without mercy until they fall dead in the fields. And the fourth is, Kill the remaining people with pick axes and pointed sticks and bayonets and rifles and plastic bags. Isn't that so, monk?"

The man's shoulders worked as he quietly sobbed, awaiting his death.

"You killed my uncle Ket and his wife and my beautiful cousins," Ding-Toy said. "Confess!"

The man shook his head and uttered a choked cry. "I don't even know who they are…"

Ding nodded savagely. "Very well. You killed the uncles and aunts and mothers and fathers and brothers and sisters of your own people, did you not?"

"Pol Pot made me do it."

"No, monk, say you chose to do it. Say, 'I wanted to do it.' Say it!"

The man looked down at the floor, his entire body trembling. "I wanted to do it," he repeated mechanically.

Ding brought down the stump with a burst of super-human fury, smashing it into the floor with such power that it shattered into pieces and broke two of his fingers with the force of the recoil. As he hunkered down on the floor and wept, he could hear the sound of foliage being hurriedly brushed aside as the man fled full speed into the forest.

~

After nearly one year in the refugee camp, Eng's name appeared on the list and the family migrated to California. On the plane, the stewardess served Ona two meals, and she could not remember being that full in many years. They lived with another Cambodian family for a couple of months until they got on their feet, renting an apartment on the third floor of a run-down three-story, flat-roofed, pink stucco building. Ding-Toy and his wife obtained jobs in a factory and Ona's daughters went to school. Eng fell into a depression and try as she might, Ona could not rouse him from it. He took English classes during the night and worked as a dishwasher in a restaurant. He struggled terribly with the language and complained he could not learn anything new. "I sleep badly at night," he said.

"Do you dream of the camps?" she asked.

"I am happy in one way," he said. "Because I feel for the first time no one is trying to kill me. Do you know what I mean?"

"Yes, of course."

"During the day it's not so bad. There's the dirty dishes to keep my mind occupied. I try to recall the new words I learn in school, saying them over and over in my mind. Then someone speaks to me and everything disappears. Nothing new sticks in my mind. Do you remember before Pol Pot sent us into the fields how good my memory was? I could remember whole conversations, passages that you read me from books, do you remember? Now everything leaves as soon as it comes."

She grasped his hand and brought it to her heart.

"The night feels so hard," he continued. "The words in my mind echo inside me and the camp comes back." His eyes filled with tears and he began to cry. "Ona, I can no longer go forward. I see other people living their lives, going here and there, in cars and buses, talking to each other, laughing, and I can't imagine how they do it. It's as if I'm watching everything from inside a bamboo cage, grasping at things I cannot reach. I can't rid myself of this feeling of death no matter how hard I try."

"Have you been drinking?"

"A little. It relaxes me."

"This is not good," she said. "The drink makes the pain go more deeply inside. Why won't you pray and meditate instead?"

"I can't pray or meditate. I don't know how you can.

My prayers are like lead in my heart and whenever I meditate I fall asleep and have bad dreams. The gods seem so far away from me now. The camp blocks out everything. I miss my brother. I miss him so much. I was sure he escaped. He must be dead. Do you suppose he is dead, Ona?"

He fell weeping into his wife's arms but continued to speak between sobs. "I dreamt last night that I was looking for my house in the forest and I was being chased by a tiger. I built a fire and I was going to jump into it before the tiger came. Then my brother appeared, telling me to be careful. What does it mean?"

"The fire is your anger and your brother is warning you not to let it go too far."

"Late at night an idea comes to me, Ona. It is hard to resist. I see myself taking a rope and hanging myself from the tree in the back of our building."

"Eng, you must overcome this suffering. After all we've been through, you speak about taking your life? That would be a grave sin. Banish those thoughts from your mind. I need you. Your children need you. I do not want you to die."

He pulled away from her and for a moment his dull eyes flashed with anger. "Ona, I dream of the camps and it is the same as if it is still happening. It goes on happening to me every day. It is as if this, what's happening, is a dream and that, what happened, is real. That is the only thing that is real. The starvation, the beatings, the torture, the sickness. I dream of things that already happened and in my dreams they are happening again with the same intensity. Do you understand?" he sobbed. "My memories taunt me. They have taken the form of the yotears, the fields, the death. I try to focus on the dishes to forget, the new words, but this exhausts me. Do you understand?"

She nodded slowly.

"You seem happy," he said. "I am happy for you. But I can't understand how it is so."

What could she possibly tell him? She didn't know what to tell herself. She, too, dreamt of the camps, but a timeless part of her watched the scenes, knowing that life reigned forever beyond death. The camp meant nothing compared to the light growing within her. Though her outer sight never fully recovered, her inner eye shone brilliantly, like the full moon on a cloudless night. Even in her sleep she could not forget the truth in which she abided. For her, there was no death.

Ona cried for her husband, wishing she could take him directly into her heart and heal his damage. But she knew that like her, like everyone, he was completely alone.

"Our suffering must mean something," she said.

"Otherwise it eats us up. I want you to live on. I need you. I love you. Your children need you. We need you to transform your suffering into something that will help you live."

Eng shook his head, the tears streaming down his cheeks. "There is nothing I can do. Pol Pot has crushed me. I am now without spirit. My spirit left my body in Cambodia."

Rocco Lo Bosco

Epilogue

The years pass, bringing Eng a slow, withering sickness. Their children have done well in their new country. Ding is a supervisor in an electronics company, Tevy is a nurse and Kunthea is finishing a Ph.D. in biology. Ona wears thick glasses. She has spent the years caring for her ruined husband, reading books printed with large type, tending her garden, and gazing upon the great shining heart that has grown within her. She has moved into a nicer apartment where a line of photographs hang on the wall above a small shrine to Buddha. The photos are of her husband and kids. It's best that she has no other photos of uncles, aunts, cousins, and of course, her brother and his family. Everyone whose likeness does not hang on the wall was killed in the fields by Pol Pot's soldiers.

On the wall where you enter the apartment is a large

wooden plaque that contains the written instructions, in finely printed red letters, to the prisoners of the Tuol Sleng Extermination Center, none of whom survived. As with the death camps of Nazi Germany, a picture was taken of the prisoner before and after death. The classrooms on the ground floor of this center were used as the torture chamber. Each room had a metal bed frame to which the prisoners were strapped and a school desk and chair for the interrogator. Today it is a museum. Ona keeps these instructions as a memorial to all who died in Cambodia.

1. You must answer in conformity with the questions I ask you. Do not turn away from my questions.
2. Don't try to escape by making pretexts according to your hypocritical ideas.
3. Don't be a fool for you are a person who dares to thwart the revolution.
4. You must immediately answer my questions without wasting time to reflect.
5. Don't tell me about your little incidents committed against propriety. Don't tell me either about the essence of the revolution.
6. During the bastinado or the electrocution you must not cry loudly.

7. Do sit down quietly. Wait for orders. If there are no orders, do nothing. If I ask you to do something, you must immediately do it without protesting.

8. Don't make any pretexts about Kampuchea Krom in order to hide your jaw of traitor.

9. If you disobey any point of my regulations, you will get either ten strokes of the whip or five shocks of electric discharge.

10. Remember at all times Kampuchea Krom acts in behalf of the greater good.

Many people have asked Ona what caused the holocaust in Cambodia. She has always answered, "There are no reasons for it. Not even one."

From a window in the kitchen she can see her vegetable garden, the rooftops of other houses, telephone wires and finally the ocean, which she calls "my beautiful cup."

A small group of Ona's friends gather at her apartment occasionally, bringing food and gifts. They come to hear her speak of the wondrous dimensions of life in which they believe and wish to remember.

It is the eve of her husband's death and her friends gather round his bedside. He lies peacefully in a bed in the corner, eyes half opened, listening while she speaks. I am not supposed to disclose her message. To do so is to cheat for she is not with you now, only I am. But I cannot resist sharing just a tiny excerpt:

Within each of us is a limitless heart. We live in a world that appears to have been here before we arrived, but in truth each of us is already a world. We encompass everything around us, the six directions and all they contain: earth, sky, sun, moon, ocean, stars, and the innumerable beings who suffer to live. The fish swim and the birds fly inside each of us. Everything we encounter as something other than ourselves is but our true self in a myriad of forms, ever changing, ever becoming. Early in our lives, we were taught a world based on what existed before us, but it is the energy of our own life that carries that world forth in time. Therefore, the shared world in which we live is not the central one. We are the central one. We are the power by which everything lives.

Our actions are important not because they will bring us personal gain or loss, but because they will either further hide or reveal the truth we are most deeply and fully. We best live when we live for the life that makes all living. Deciding to do this, we will act accordingly, reaching out in compassion to the lives that surround us.

What is it? the mind asks. What are you talking

about? I can't see it. I can't touch it. I can't hear it. I can't smell it. I can't taste it. I can't think it. How can I know it? And you might say, "Oh yes, it might be something I can't see." And so you go on with that kind of thinking, looking for something you cannot see as if you might see it. As if you're looking for yet another object. But what I am speaking about is never an object. It can never be second to anything.

Do you want what I am saying to be true? Maybe you think that if what I'm saying is true, your suffering has meaning and everything will turn out okay. Only this is not the case. It is up to you to make your suffering mean something. If not, you live without meaning, for the meaning of your life comes first from your suffering. Our suffering shapes our existence. Even the flower suffers to open its petals so that you may see its beauty. Even the stars suffer in their burning so that you may see them. Your suffering is yours and yours only. And you must decide what to do with what belongs to you. You must decide. What will you do with your suffering once you realize how much it belongs to you? How will it affect your relationship with the other?

There is no way around the pure life of which I speak, extremely subtle and always hidden to the restless mind. And this is the great tragedy of humanity, that it forgets this changeless reality and yet seeks it continually in the realm of change—clinging to territory, wealth, power, positions. Trying to make the world into an idea of possession. All around you can witness the simple truth of what I say. People everywhere are driven to seek. Some seek money, others status, others knowledge, others love, others destruction, and to these things they tenaciously cling. This is the way of sorrow.

Don't think the power of you is far away. It lies waiting just beyond your next thought, your next breath, your next heartbeat. It lies waiting silently in the silence you cover up with the noise of your days and the dreaming of your nights. When you realize this power your heart becomes gentle. You express knowledge of it as non-violence.

The greatest expression of knowledge is non-violence. The knower does not wish to harm any living thing in thought, word, or deed. Not because one is afraid to hurt. Not because one was told not to hurt. Not because it is the right thing to do. But because one knows that it is impossible to hurt another without harming one's relationship with one's very own life.

Stop ignoring it. Sit still. Turn inward in prayer and meditation. Consider the heart. It has been subjected to such indifference and brutality. It has been taught how to die, not live. The heart must empty itself of grief. The heart must be silent and alert. Then the secret will be revealed. Learn again to think with the heart and give with the heart, no matter how many times you have been hurt. Don't hide the heart like a turtle pulling in its head for fear of being trampled. Only a heart that knows pain can sing, only a heart that knows pain can care. Live in your heart, think with your mind, serve with your body. You must cry, you must laugh, you must live this life, this life that never ends. Taste it and be filled with it. To liberate the heart is the greatest of all human challenges. Spread your heart out. It will not hurt. It is very strong. The whole world is in it: the sky, the ocean, all living beings, all you fear, and all you love.

See what I mean? It was wrong to repeat what she said for she is not here saying it to you herself. Her argument can be overturned in the wink of an eye. Why? So much has been said in the world, so much printed, so much discussed, so much analyzed, that nothing is true anymore. We've come to the end of truth. We have only its remainder left: technique. Only fools can envision life without war, murder, rape, and destruction. A world without a constant apocalypse. It would be easier to believe in an invisible sun.

Yet, when I stand near her, her words enter me, her voice, her peace. For that time, I know she speaks truth.

∾

Right now she is sitting by her kitchen window with a cup of tea, gazing at her garden, furrowed and damp in late spring. The bodies grow like mountains within her, and in the background she always hears the sound of the porcelain furnace cooking humanity in its fiery depths. Yet she cannot forget. She is the light of the soaring bird who never rests. She is the rain, the tree, the rooftop, and the star. She looks upon the angels and the demons with an equal eye.

A sea of hands tear another day in half. A desert of mouths call for more. Ona smiles in thirstless peace.

And I stand in her garden and she smiles at me.

Spring's Black Buddha

Your serenity in this morning's spring mist
changes nothing, for the sunrise
blazing in the hedges above your head
is also the sunset of the death card.
I see a man and a woman at play
in the field of ruin,
Romeo and Juliet
stranded in last winter's kitchen
sharing a dry crust of bread
and steaming a pot of ice.

The fire eye,
the diamond heart,
even the golden letter
fall into a bottomless well

of longing that is
stronger than death itself.

O Buddha cloaked in the black
stone of your skin,
enfolded in the silence of your dark heart,
the white ash spread round you,
the solitary bird of anguish
has been singing
since the flower of the world first opened.
Lift your hands from their
brilliant stillness
and take my three offerings:
this battered cup,
this circus horse of desire,
this ruined love that will not die.
And I will do my work,
bearing witness to the emerald bud
breaking through the hardwood of winter.
I will sweep the tears of spring off the porch.
I will praise this unending day
that has begun once again.